BODY OF OPINION

'This third collaboration by a female twosome has likable Supt. Robert Bone of Tunbridge Wells looking after his daughter Cha since the car smash that killed his wife and baby, looking – with reciprocated affection – at Cha's attractive teacher Grizel, and looking into the bizarre shooting of another attractive woman in a rock idol's bedroom during an all-night party . . . The sterling plot is warmed by a tender humanity and spiced with not a little excellent wit, starting at the title'
The Sunday Times

'Captivating . . . This duo's Superintendent Bone must rank as one of the more human plods now on the fictional beat'
The Guardian

Jill Staynes and Margaret Storey first met at St Paul's Girls' School where they wrote bizarre serials. One went to Oxford and advertising, the other to Cambridge and secretarial work in publicity. After some happy years teaching, they are now devoting all their time to the pleasure of writing.

Also by Staynes and Storey

GOODBYE, NANNY GRAY
A KNIFE AT THE OPERA

and published by Corgi Books

BODY OF OPINION

Staynes & Storey

CORGI BOOKS

BODY OF OPINION

A CORGI BOOK   0552 13470 8

Originally published in Great Britain by The Bodley Head Ltd.

PRINTING HISTORY
The Bodley Head edition published 1988
Corgi edition published 1989

This book is set in 11/12½ Bembo by Goodfellow & Egan Ltd.,
Cambridge

Corgi Books are published by Transworld Publishers Ltd., 61–63
Uxbridge Road, Ealing, London W5 5SA, in Australia by Transworld
Publishers (Australia) Pty. Ltd., 15–23 Helles Avenue, Moorebank,
NSW 2170, and in New Zealand by Transworld Publishers (N.Z.)
Ltd., Cnr. Moselle and Waipareira Avenues, Henderson, Auckland.

Printed and bound in Great Britain by
Cox & Wyman Ltd, Reading

CHAPTER ONE

Lamia noticed that the glass in her hand was trembling, and she put it down quickly on the mantelshelf, a nasty Tudor affair in carved stone. Her other hand tightly held an appropriately named clutch bag, in black satin with a diamanté trim. In it, she was carrying all a woman could need at a party where she hoped to meet her husband's girl-friend: compact, mirror, comb, lipstick and gun. She allowed the conversation, mainly concerned with time-share apartments in the Algarve and the difficulty of getting someone's teenage son to sit his A-levels while on heroin, to wash over her while she scanned the crowd. Ken Cryer, whose party it was, had no silly inhibitions as to playing his own music at it, and a track from his latest album *For Crying Out Loud* trashed everyone's eardrums as they shouted nothings at each other. She hoped somebody would point the woman out to her before long.

Ken, upstairs in his son's bedroom over the porch, was saying, 'Dr Walsh's machine reports he's out to dinner; I left a message, but we're very unlikely to see him before morning. How is it now?'

'It's quiet now. It's all right, Dad, I keep telling you. It's just the bug all the others had.'

'I don't give a tinker's for all the others, mate.'

Jem grinned, pleased at his father's concern. They were much alike; although Jem at thirteen lacked the lines, the harshness, he had the alert eyes and the tousled, mousy hair.

'What makes me *more* sick is missing the party.'

'You've got the noise of it. I hadn't realized how it sounds up here. I'll get it turned—'

'I was brought up on that noise. I like it. Cradle music.'

Ken put his hand once more on Jem's clammy brow. The noise, of music and voices competing, made them speak loudly even here, and the persistent r'n'b drum came through the fabric.

'I'll get it turned down.'

'Don't do that. I haven't a headache now. It's just the tum.'

An increase of noise: the door opened to the cosy chic of Ken's secretary, a big girl making no concessions to her size in a long, glittering, sequined jacket over her long, black dress.

'Sorry, Ken. Noel Prestbury's detonating. Can you come?'

'God. Okay. I'll be back, Jem; I'll look in.'

'Don't worry.'

Ken passed Edwina and hared for the stairs. Jem let their voices and footsteps merge with the sound and then, bundling his duvet round him, he left his bed. Crouched on a large wooden chest in a corner of the passage he wrapped the duvet round him and peered through a narrow squinch window into the big room below. He saw the focus of attention, a blonde whose hair flowed over the shoulders of her gold frock, and the grey head of the man berating her. He looked to see his father arrive; but a swift, urgent pang prevented him from seeing any more – erupting from his cocoon he fled for his bathroom.

Ken, making his way to the epicentre, saw the girl, a little smile on her face under the sweep of hair. Mel Rees, Ken's minder, stood trying to intervene politely.

'—inaccurate and obscene. Blasphemous balder-dash—'

There was hope on the staring faces all around, hope for trouble, hope for the scene to come to blows. Prestbury's violence incited rather than embarrassed.

'—Damned disgraceful. I wrote to your editor—' the voice, one of hard ranting energy that matched the flushed face, changed gear and rode into hysteria. 'Take a horsewhip to you if I would ever strike a woman, smirking, filthy, atheist bitch.'

Prestbury, opening and clenching his fists, quivering before lift-off, might, if offered a horse-whip by some charitable hand at this moment, have used it regardless of any thought of gender.

Yet he seemed almost grateful to be led away, as if he had not known how to deal with her provo-cation. Ken soothed, offered a fresh drink, listened with grave attention to the incoherent account of how Prestbury's hospitality had been abused, his faith insulted. The manner of insult was not clear but Ken, from his own experience of the man, knew Prestbury for a militant Catholic, one who

7

had campaigned for the Tridentine Mass and had bitterly criticized the Pope for abolishing it; who had announced his desire to go to Rome and shoot the damned heathen who tried to assassinate the present Pope.

'Showed her the whole house, Cryer. Spent an afternoon with her, answering every tomfool question. She seemed genuinely interested – I showed her the Chapel. That was the real mistake.' The sturdy toothbrush of a moustache trembled. 'Told her about the Host being removed; not allowed to be reserved any more.'

'Reserved?' Ken's mind produced only the idea of tickets. He poured more gin, steadying Prestbury's glass with his free hand. Get him incapable, quietly under a table somewhere.

'Reserved. Kept in the Chapel.' Prestbury darted a choleric glance at Ken under the folds of his eyelids. 'Shouldn't have to tell *you* about that.'

'No. Sorry.'

'For a hundred years it's been there, until – I told that bitch the whole story and she, she saw how much it meant to me and she made fun of it. She wrote it all up in her vile little article as a *joke*.'

'Not her article, Noel. She's only Hervey's assistant. He does the writing.'

'But she did the telling. She told it to him like that – you saw her smirk. Damned pleased at what she did.'

Ken inwardly admitted it. 'She's not the writer, though.'

'And I'd told my friends when it was to be published. Expected an appreciation of the place.'

'Noel, listen. I've not read the thing myself but I'll bet your friends know better. You don't think people who know you will pay attention to crap like that.'

'All the people who *don't* know the place. It's damnable!' He rumbled on, less audibly. Ken thought it was all a bit Brideshead. Still, he sympathized, detachedly, and made a resolve that, after all, he would not have the Manor written up in Alex Hervey's *Serendips*, as Hervey's letter had suggested.

'Never forgive it!' Prestbury's small, bright eyes shot a final glance at Ken. He turned away.

Ken could move on. He passed Edwina, who was laughing seismically, showing the neat little teeth and dimples. Her mirror jacket was not constructed to minimize her happy bulk but heliographed Nature's generosity to the room; earrings like infant chandeliers danced, and her smiling face had the perfect, innocently curved features of a Victorian china doll. Ken ran a finger round her hips under the hem of the jacket, and she trod back with a soft slipper onto his foot.

'Is it fun being Ken's secretary?' Fiona Herne asked. 'Or absolutely deadly? I've often wondered.'

'So have I.' Edwina glanced at him over her shoulder. 'The worst is when you want him to read or sign something, and you can race after him all day like trying to catch a lift on Concorde.'

She laughed again, and Ken moved slowly away, smiling, his eyes on the watch for empty glasses, for people stranded. There was Mick

9

Parsons, on the periphery of a group, but Ken was not about to rescue that one. He might be Gwyn Griffiths' latest gofer and props man, but in Ken's book he was superfluous, an invitation wangler, a chancer; the mouth too mobile, too obliging, the eyes too watchful.

There was one of those moments of suspended life when a tape gives out and someone puts in the next one. The comparative silence produced laughter, an easy warm laughter gratifying to a host.

He came up with Sutton Somerton and Mary Highmountain, and this juxtaposition pleased him too. Sutton appeared more uneasy than ever, and his customary face was that of a man sure there is something deeply wrong happening quite near. Probably he was not used to women as tall as he was, and Mary was at least as tall; she was also Cherokee and fiercely beautiful, in a soft black leather jumpsuit.

'Don't tell me you're a guitarist,' she said. Affront joined the manic wariness in Somerton's eyes but his mouth smiled.

'Why, do I look like one?'

She shrugged, a displacement the jumpsuit only just allowed.

'I can see you on stage, but you're not a singer.'

Ken agreed. Sutton hadn't the looks, the image, for a frontman. Of course, Mary's employer set rather high standards.

'I'm an architect. I converted Cryer's studio here – it was a barn, a scheduled building. We had to keep the structure, which I managed, of course.'

He spoke complacently. Clearly the barn had much to thank him for.

'Of *course*,' said Mary Highmountain.

He tried attack. 'What do *you* do?' He leant forward with exaggerated interest.

'I mind Archangel.'

'I beg your pardon?' He came upright, deeply baffled. 'With this noise going on, I don't think I heard you.'

She almost smiled, not an indulgence she was given to, and turning she indicated with one long brown finger; and the man with white hair, although across the room and surrounded by people, turned to look at her. Ken wondered at this *rapport*. He was totally without envy of Archangel's extraordinary face, and merely reflected that it was fortunate in having a hardness that denied effeminacy and raised it to beauty.

'That is Archangel,' Mary said.

'Oh yes. Yes. I know the face, of course.'

'Of course.'

Somerton's interest in Archangel was as minimal as it was in any other subject not connected with himself, and he scanned the room, gave her an empty smile and said, 'Excuse me. Someone I've got to talk to.'

Mary said to Ken as Somerton made his way off into the throng, 'And aren't we sorry?'

'You're a hard woman.'

They crossed through the crowd in the other direction, to talk to Archangel. At Mary's approach, another minder, of the more conventional fifteen-stone kind, casually and irresistibly moved off with a wide-eyed girl who had been hanging round, staring at Archangel, who had dealt kindly with her efforts long enough. Mary assumed the blocking position, although she let the golden Alix Hamilton slide into the group. The little smile that had so exacerbated Prestbury's temper was still on her lips. She said 'Ha*llo*,' to Archangel, offering her cheek. He kissed it.

'Hallo, my sweet.'

They exchanged glances; Ken thought they shared some private joke. He wanted to introduce his neighbour, Fiona Herne, to Archangel – she made jewellery and delicate ornaments – and he went to find her. One of the loud tracks had come over the speakers now, and the lights had dimmed a little; he could not locate her. One of his minders located him, however: the doctor had arrived.

Monro Walsh had a genial grimness about him. He narrowed his eyes at the noise, and Ken saved explanations until they were upstairs. In the passage light, Walsh's saturnine face showed fatigue.

'I see. Well, leave me with Jemmy. I'll come and report. No, you've your guests to see to.'

All the same, Ken went with him to Jem's room, where Jem, though wan, clearly wanted no fuss of parental hovering. Ken stated, 'Well, I'll be downstairs, then,' and neither of them said him nay. As he went, he straightened the 'Private' sign on his bedroom door, and checked it was locked, although he knew it was. He ran downstairs into the uproar. One of Archangel's stylish songs was usurping the air, and to its irresistible beat Ken drew Edwina to dance.

Dr Walsh, covering up Jemmy's stomach after a careful palpation, said, 'You chose a poor time and place to be ill. This noise – appalling.'

'No, it's great. Now I've thrown up I don't have a headache, much. I'm only mad I can't be down there and *in* it. But I've still got the squitters and my legs feel all weird. I thought it was the world's best luck when school broke up early. Sorry for the blokes who'd got the bug, but all the same it meant I'd be home for Dad's party. *And* it was yah-boo-sucks to him because he'd arranged it just so I wouldn't be here. And look what happens. The Bug Strikes.'

He produced a wan effort at a grin. Walsh alleviated his dark expression for Jem's benefit, and it became marginally less odd that he should be a successful G.P.

The room was above the porch and hall, so that a mullioned bay formed one end of it. It had a small fireplace with a hob; a cavernous basket chair, and an oak chest; a shelf-desk with a typist's chair on castors, the seat and back adjusted for Jem's thirteen-year-old frame; and along the shelf above the crammed bookcase was a collection of stones – quartzes, onyx, serpentine, malachite, iron pyrites, copper ore, amber; on one wall, an ikon, a small traditional one hanging on its own, then a board full of pictures, postcards, cutouts; pinned out on the panelling opposite, a Japanese butterfly kite in splendour. Almost invisible among the bedclothes a worn animal known as Thred Bear lurked.

Walsh sat on the bed. 'Well, you'll live,' he said. 'Any more trouble with the leg?'

'Oh no. Except, it's really weird, I know when the weather's going to change. Not an ache, just a feeling all inside, like it was too full.'

'After a really spectacular break like that, you do get some sensitivity.' They talked of it for a while. Then Walsh stood up and, with a nod that Jem knew was friendly, he left him.

The door of Ken Cryer's room was open, although when they came upstairs Cryer had told him it was kept locked during parties – 'Plenty of bonking-space elsewhere' – and Walsh glanced in, ready to give Cryer a status report on Jem's insides, but it was not Cryer moving about in front of the big looking-glass. After an intent, sombre stare, Walsh went in.

Ken Cryer, at the happy stage of knowing it's worthwhile giving a party, but anxious to see Walsh about Jemmy, knowing Archangel had to leave soon and wanting to talk more to him – flying in early just for this party should have more recognition – went through the throng. Sutton Somerton was telling someone else that he'd converted the barn for Ken. He looked overturned, more manic. His information was being shouted above the amps' production and was not being received with enthusiasm. Ken diagnosed terminal boredom, decided Somerton needn't be asked to any further social events, and moved in, saying, 'Fiona! Archangel's got to go soon. He's seen one of your creations—'

Somerton said, leaning over her affably, 'What do *you* create? Frocks, is it?'

She smiled with creditable sweetness. 'Oh no. Expensive tat. Jewels, and things. It really wouldn't interest you.'

'No, really—' but Ken bore Fiona away.

Archangel's looks were not impaired by proximity, or even by that most dangerous of facial activities, smiling. 'Oh *yes*,' he said, effortlessly heard through the music. 'I've been thinking of getting a close friend of mine garrotted for the sake of your Rain Tree that he's been flaunting. Are you wholly booked out or can I filter in a commission for, say, an earring for Drinking Fountain here,' with a hand on the tall minder's shoulder, 'and something of the nature of Rain Tree except that I naturally want it to be entirely different.'

Fiona's elegant coolness had warmed. She said, 'I can send you drawings—'

A hand touched Archangel's sleeve, and he turned towards his secretary's hornrims. 'Sure, sure, untwist the knickers.'

The secretary was heard to utter 'Wembley,' and Archangel patted him and turned back to Fiona.

'I should get some sleep in before the sound check; it's Wembley tomorrow, or tonight it must be by now. Drawings; please. Henry will later today send you addresses where I'll be, and . . .' He began to move out to the hall, taking Fiona, and Ken followed . . . 'I'll call from New York the day after tomorrow, let you know the parameters, is that right?'

Monro Walsh was hovering in the hall. Ken put a hand on his arm. 'Shan't be a minute, but Archangel's leaving.'

'I'm in something of a hurry,' Walsh said. 'I've had a message Edwina just gave me, from a patient, and I wanted to—'

'Ken?' from the front door.

'Sorry, I have to—'

Archangel, his secretary, his minders, an extraneous girl Ken hadn't spoken to, in a dress like a very decorative table napkin and not much bigger, all ducked into the huge silver car and it swirled away. In the lobby by the door Mel Rees, Ken's security man, watched on the closed-circuit TV and opened the gates. Ken turned to speak to Monro Walsh and found he had gone. His Cortina took off after the silver car, mundane compared with that space rocket. Ken, who knew him fairly well, was sorry to have annoyed him; and ran upstairs to check with Jem before hurrying back to the party. Edwina waved to him, scintillating across the room. From here on the step he could see all the gyrating and weaving; an exhilarating, good-party roar deafened him. He leant to shift the dimmer switch further down, then joined the crowd and made his way through, found Edwina and a drink simultaneously, kissed her and drank. He put a hand on the metallic chill of her sequins and waited for the warmth to come through. She moved, very slightly, into the curve of his arm.

An hour later the party had assumed the devastated air of happy exhaustion. The rooms seemed to have enlarged, not because of the few departures, but because the level of humanity had subsided, onto sofas, cushions, the floor. Ken had turned down the stereo to match the muting of voices. Fiona Herne came down into the room, her body relaxed, her eyes sleepy. She glanced at Ken and slightly smiled.

The innumerable family of Ken's Indonesian cook reappeared with trays of small dishes of food, with coffee. Someone asked if there was tea, a diffident enquiry met with pleasure – of course there was tea; how would Madam like it? A magnum of champagne also appeared, borne by Pak Sim himself, and was opened by Ken with the first audible cork-popping of this night, scoring a wall-ceiling-wall cannon shot with the cork and raising a cheer. Ken sat down and knew from the sensation in his back and knees that he hadn't sat down for hours. He looked round, and wondered how many people had come whom he hadn't invited; for instance he hadn't invited Mick Parsons, who seemed to have left. Griffiths must have brought him along. Nor Anne Somebody, who'd also gone; she'd come with Somerton, who now sat with his long legs crooked up and his head down, his arms propped on his knees and a champagne glass dangling. The golden Alix Hamilton must be upstairs with someone. Jay Tansley-Ferrars had brought her as she wanted to 'write up' the Manor, or her employer Alex Hervey did. Ken was not going to stand for that after what the two of them seemed to have done to Prestbury.

His drummer, Si Worth, came down into the room (from the loo? from Fiona Herne?), dropped at Edwina's side and reclined at ease. The party hadn't much longer to run, but it had run very well.

By the time the final lingerers had been persuaded

to go either home or to bed here, Ken was tired. He said to Si, 'I begin to know I'm not twenty-five any more. I'd have gone straight through and then into next day's work.'

'With a little chemical help,' Si recalled.

Their feet trod the stairs. 'And I'm more knackered than after a concert. Not got the high from an audience.'

However, there was bed waiting. He looked in at Jem, who was asleep. Even in Jem's curtained room, dark appreciably was giving way to soft grey around the windows. Ken returned to the main landing, got out his keys and found the one for his bedroom door. It did not turn. He took the handle and found the door was open.

It annoyed him. He had locked it, and knew he had. He'd even tested it earlier on. Now he would find his bed messed – tumbled and damp, and the quilt perhaps soiled. The light came on under his hand. He saw the curtains of his four-poster half drawn, and it annoyed him afresh that whoever had got in hadn't after all pulled the quilt back and so must have – Ken strode to the bed and swept the curtain back at the bedhead. The table lamp shone on Alix Hamilton, sitting up against the heaped pillows, soft gold of her hair gleaming on the harsher gold of her dress. She had drawn the bedspread up to her waist; her hands, slightly covered by the arum-lily sleeves, lay on her thighs. She gazed straight ahead, smiling a little.

'No,' Ken said. 'Sorry, but definitely no.' He took a handful of the quilt and yanked it off her. She toppled towards him. *Stoned*, he thought, *Oh*

18

hell, as he automatically caught her and pushed her upright.

He felt a warm slime on his hand and flung her from him in a reaction of disgust; but his hand was smeared red. He could smell both the metallic thread of her dress and then another dislikeable smell he did not recognize. He could see the hole in her side.

He backed away across the room, stood a moment looking at the bed, at his hand. He retched; put the back of his clean left hand to his mouth. He had to get his keys out of his right trouser pocket with his left hand and lock the door . . .

CHAPTER TWO

Birds had got the day going in full song as the cars drew up and unloaded gear and men in the steadily increasing light. Robert Bone wished he felt half their zest; a quarter would do. The phone call had caught him going back to bed with a mouth full of peppermint magnesia pills while his guts panged. He had put the pill bottle in his pocket, left the usual note for his daughter . . . and here was the pathologist Ferdy Foster, casting him a morose brown regard. Ferdy, like Bone, preferred to be on the spot himself and not wait for things to be brought to him. His face, a miracle of erosion, was not flattered by this light. 'Damn birds,' he said, in his gravelly drawl.

The door opened. They had come, as requested, round the house to a side door because Cryer's young son, who was ill, slept over the front door. Cryer scanned them and his hard dissipated face almost smiled. 'Nice it's you,' he said to Bone . . .

They followed him upstairs.

The team went in first, like a decontamination squad, the flash camera fizzing and flaring. Bone saw through the doorway the panelled room, the four-poster bed with its patterned curtains and quilt and valance. He watched as they dealt with carpets, bed-clothes, furniture. He was thankful that the scene-of-crime officer was Detective-Inspector Steve Locker. He had been working with Blane, who did not know him and was apt to resent his presence. Bone surreptitiously ate another tablet.

The woman lay back askew on the pillows, hair spread, eyes open as though studying some menacing secret embroidered on the tester. Her face was Garbo-ish, sculptured, with strong planes, blanching in the flash. He thought, not for the first time, how curiously lacking in something a dead body was, how obvious that something had been subtracted; a wonder that people could doubt the existence of the spirit. She was beautiful still.

They found, and photographed, the small metal cylinders ejected by the shots, and they dropped them in bags. They found them by the bedside table and under the foot of the bed.

Eventually he could beckon Ken, from the landing window-seat where he was talking to Simon Worth, and ask how the woman was found. Someone still beavered in the bathroom.

'Her name's Alix Hamilton. I don't know her at all. She works for Alexander Hervey, his research assistant. He writes these articles on old houses. Well, I came in, I was furious that the door was open and I'd locked it to keep out the crowd. There's beds everywhere, I wanted this one left alone. The quilt should be in a museum I suppose. I'm a vandal to sleep under it but you've got to believe a bloke, I never thought of anyone getting murdered in it.'

Bone saw Cryer's change of expression as it

dawned on him that *you've got to believe* could be taken in another way, that he was himself a suspect. Bone did not think it easy to put on that precise look if one were guilty, and he was relieved to be able to suppose that Ken, whom he knew a little – he had dined here – was probably not. Mel Rees stood by the door, looming slightly as a man of his useful bulk was bound to do. Another, larger and black, looked in, spoke to Mel and went away.

'I think I pushed this drawer. Can I touch?'

'It's all been dusted.'

'I keep a gun here. It's licensed, and normally the drawer's locked, but I've had death threats and lately I've had some from a nutter with religion—' he turned and indicated a chest where candlesticks stood; and froze.

'It's gone. Did your men take anything from there? It's a monstrance, Italian, seventeenth century. Look, that may be what some of this is about. I can't see what *she's* got to do with it but – oh God, it was lovely. A beautiful thing, a sunburst round a crystal circle, not very big but just—' his hands moved outwards – 'beautiful.'

Bone, really sorry for this loss, taking in the fact of theft, was distracted by the state of his own insides and the necessity of getting Cryer back to the main subject of concern. As Cryer turned to him, he pointed at the bed.

'Yes. Of course.' Ken rubbed his eyes. 'Of course that's more important. I'm not thinking straight. I'm tired. Used to be able to stay awake three nights in a row once, when I was on drugs. I

22

was really plugged into the mains then, and now a sleepless night runs the batteries right down. Crystals definitely drained, Mr Bone.' He looked so weary that Bone felt sympathy, an emotion overtaken by a seismic pang from his stomach. Cryer was talking from nerves.

Steve Locker stood waiting. Bone said, 'Ken, Steve is in charge here. He has to know exactly how you found everything.'

What Bone found was a bathroom, most likely Jem's. He felt improved when he came out.

They told him Cryer was downstairs. He took a final look at the bedroom, where Foster was at work, and after a word with Steve he went down the oak flight. Cryer, emerging from the kitchen regions, said, 'There'll be breakfast before long. It looks like a Calcutta sidewalk in there,' jerking his head towards the kitchen. 'Pak Sim's family all sleeping off the cooking wine among the dishes. Once they get going, though, no one'd know there'd been a party. They're wanting to start, but I told them everything's held up until word from your lot.'

An Indonesian came out with a tray of coffee. From his crumpled trousers and immaculate jacket, he had slept in the one and hung the other up neatly.

Bone sipped the coffee, dubious about its effect on his turbulent digestion. The effect on Cryer was to lighten, even seem to erase, the lines on his face. As he drank it off, his quilted black silk jacket parted to reveal a teeshirt eerily printed with his likeness. The face on his chest stared cynically at Bone.

The main room had a wrecked air, the floor

covered with cushions, glasses, dishes, rucked rugs; a curtain had been partly torn down.

'Wonder how that happened?' Ken said idly. 'Violent games. How soon can Pak Sim's lot clear up in here? They want to get back to their work in London.'

'We'll have to talk to them all.'

'Some of them speak English,' Ken said.

Moving on, they disturbed a young man asleep on a sofa in the next room, who sluggishly hauled himself round to look. Ken said, 'Meet the police,' and the boy said, 'Christ, is this a drugs bust?' making Bone wonder if it ought to be. Locker was at their heels and impounded the boy for questions.

A large, very pretty blonde girl caught up with them and said, 'There'll be breakfast in ten minutes in the library; for other ranks, in the brown room in half an hour.'

'Ta, love. Super, this is Edwina Marsh, my secretary. It's a mystery to me how I ever did without her; shambled through life somehow.'

She was dressed in a longish black skirt, a man's black shirt yellow-striped, over it, and a long black cotton jacket. Her handshake was warm and firm, her teeth small and fine. She turned to Ken once more. 'How about hot chocolate?'

'Oh no.'

'Something with sugar in it. You're shivering.'

'I can bear sugar in coffee.' He gave her his cup, kissed her cheek, and walked on towards the library hugging himself. They sat down in the big comfortable room, whose bookshelves had proliferated to the ceiling since Bone was last here, but whose

24

sofas were as welcoming. Bone, however, opted for an upright Queen Anne chair, from a feeling that sofas at this hour would prove soporific.

'These death threats,' he said. He had to consider that it was in Cryer's bed that the body had been found, Cryer's bedroom that had been broken into.

'Letters. These recent ones were all on ordinary white paper and typed, and anonymous unless *The Brown Brother* counts as a name. They were about the monstrance.' Cryer's face contracted at the thought of his loss.

'What did you do with them?'

'Junked them.'

'A pity. How many people knew about the monstrance? That you had it, and where it was kept?'

'It was mentioned in passing in a piece in *Country Life*. Anyway this Brown Brother objected to a holy object being in secular hands and particularly the obscene hands of a pop star.'

'You'll have to tell me what a monstrance is. This one is a gold sunburst round a crystal centre.'

'The crystal's for displaying Communion bread. I gather it can be carried on a pole in procession or stand on an altar. It stood on that chest in my room. I'd a sudden wild hope it might just have got moved and your men would find it, but your Inspector Locker said no trace. I've photographs of it for security, and I wrote the postcode under it with a thingummy pen, which may be sacrilegious but everything here is marked that way.'

'And a very good idea.'

25

Edwina was back, with a quart-sized teapot, and followed by an elderly Indonesian with a tray.

'Ed, the Superintendent will want to see the photographs of the monstrance. And it seems it's a pity I junked the poison-pen epistles to the heathen.'

'I did a rescue job on them,' she said calmly, handing him a large mug of coffee. 'They're in a file in my office. I'll bring them. Why the photographs?'

'It's gone.' He looked up at her and she paused.

'Oh Ken. I'm sorry.'

He gave a rueful grimace, and drank.

She brought buff folders with the letters, the photographs, and she set out breakfast on the long table. She combined, deftly, the appearance of a china doll with that of a chic teddy bear. Also with the folders was a photocopy of the party guest list.

'I made half a dozen copies just now. Mr Locker has them.'

Bone had been looking over the letters – one torn in two, another crumpled. There were three, and they suggested an educated, intemperate person, with a masculine turn of phrase that bore out the 'Brother' with which two of them were signed. Their content added up to: unless Cryer restored the object to a place of sanctity he was doomed. The first letter merely called him an atheist, a posturing mountebank, a fornicator, an upstart social climber, an unworthy, filthy-handed sinner, and an ape. The second threatened the vengeance of God by the hand of man, and called him a heathen, a prancing blasphemer, a fornicator, a foul evil-liver and a defiler of the sacred. The third said that unless

26

the monstrance, the Abode of God, were placed in a sanctified house of prayer, Cryer would die. The writer would see that he did and no bodyguard would avail him.

'Nasty blow to the pride of my security blokes,' Cryer said as Bone put the last one down.

'M'm. You threw these away.'

'I did. I thought about the matter a bit. But after all there's no holy bread in the monstrance. And I don't keep a portrait in it or anything unsuitable. I thought, no, he hasn't a case. A nutter pure and simple.'

He did not seem to have thought that a nutter, pure and simple, would be more likely to carry out death threats than those who did have a case.

Ken was helping himself to sausages and fried bread. Bone stayed with tea and dry toast, his stomach being in a frugal mood.

'I'll take these letters, if I may.'

'You're more than welcome. You don't think someone thought that poor girl in the bed was me?'

'All possibilities have to be considered. Rationality has very often got nothing to do with crimes of violence.'

'Suppose not. Ah, the guest list. Though these were the invited guests . . . I see Ed's put others at the bottom. God, that girl is so efficient.' Ken's spatulate finger indicated names as he went on. '*He* brought a friend who stank of Press a mile off. Ed and Mel talked to him and saw him off quietly. This one brought a girl he'd just met, but she was all right. She spent the evening gazing goofily at Archangel. This is him, Mark Serafin, and these are his crew; they left before the end – he's at Wembley tonight and New York tomorrow.'

He's at Wembley gave Bone a freakish picture of the singer as footballer. He knew Archangel from Cha's bedroom wall where his picture appeared frequently along with Bono, Bowie, Annie Lennox, Jagger, and others Bone had not learnt to identify.

'About what time did they leave? Was Alix Hamilton around after they left?'

'God, I can't say. You're well into the improbability factor there; though I think Archangel knew Alix Hamilton.'

'Something they said.'

'He kissed her cheek when they met. They're both spectacular. I think they danced together.'

The far door opened and Jem Cryer came in, pale, in dressing gown and green pyjamas. His eyes were huge with excited interest and he came up to his father almost prancing.

'You shouldn't be out of bed.' Cryer pointed a half sausage on his fork.

'With all that kerfuffle going on? What's happened? Good morning, Mr Bone. Someone's died, haven't they?' He offered his hand. 'What did they die of?' He obviously hoped it wasn't old age.

'Presumably,' Bone said, 'from being shot. Mr Cryer, may I ask Jem if he heard anything like a shot?'

'You have asked him. In so many words. I see that's an official request, however, since I've

28

suddenly become *Mr Cryer*. Though believe you me, he'd have told you by now if he had. James, tell the nice policeman.'

Bone smiled – an action to which he was not much given and which he was not aware transformed his rather bleak features.

'Well, I didn't. Dr Walsh gave me some sort of settler, which has absolutely worked, but I zoomed off to sleep in all that terrific row and slept till just now.' He put a long arm over his father's shoulder and took a sausage. When Cryer turned on him, he was on the sofa innocently chewing. Cryer turned back, lifted the hotplate cover, speared himself another sausage, and said to Bone, 'Nothing much wrong with him. You'd better apply to Dr Walsh on your own account. And I didn't hear a shot either. I don't think I'd have heard even low-flying aircraft last night; and around here we get Harrier jets at roof level. I've wondered what would happen if they hit a flock of geese on the wing.'

'They're really scary,' Jem said. 'You feel like your heart would stop when they come POWEE out of nowhere. But anyway, if I did hear anything I'd have thought it was a champagne cork. They kept going all evening and they sound just like Mel's automatic.'

Edwina put cereal and coffee on a Pembroke table beside Jem. They were clearly on good terms, for she tweaked his hair and he grinned at her.

'The brat was meant to have missed the party,' Ken said. 'His school officially breaks up

29

tomorrow. But what do they do but send them home early because of this outbreak of plague, and I can't cancel everything when Jem succumbs. Monro Walsh came to see Jem late last night. He's our doctor, very decent man if a bit intense.'

Bone wrote *Dr Monro Walsh* on the list and *Jem* in brackets. Edwina refilled Ken's cup, and as she put it down he reached for it and their hands touched. His closed momentarily on hers.

'Alix Hamilton's not on the first list,' Bone commented. 'Who brought her along?'

'Jay Tansley-Ferrars. She'd been to see me about writing up the Manor – appointment made by her employer Hervey, who writes what I find are snide articles about country houses; and I think she wanted to consolidate the business, make sure I would go along with it.'

Bone put J. T-F. against Alix Hamilton's name.

'Then this other woman came with Sutton Somerton; she only said she was "Anne". We reckoned they'd had a row, as she brought him in her car but she swept off without him. He'll still be here. Breakfasting in the brown room, I suppose.'

Ferdy Foster came round the door, his somewhat mournful face questing. 'Thought I smelt coffee,' he said, and pulled his spectacles down the better to see over the top of them. 'No, I won't stay. Thank you, my dear, a cup would be mollifying. Well, Super, you haven't got a murdered woman on your hands after all.'

Bone thought: not suicide at that angle of shot.

30

Death from shock? That's what everybody dies of.

Foster's gaze swept over their faces – puzzled, relieved, alert with interest, blank. He wagged his head.

'She's a man.'

CHAPTER THREE

'Nobody's perfect,' Ken murmured.

Bone swiftly in professional detachment scanned the degree of astonishment all round. Edwina's little teeth showed as a cat's when disturbed at its laundry, her eyes huge and blank. Jem's eyebrows had lifted under his mousy thatch, Cryer put down his loaded fork, more amused than surprised.

Ferdy was watchful too. His eyes now met Bone's and he nodded significantly.

'Lamé is slippery stuff and the team don't bag and tag with modesty in mind. Wigs can come unfixed. Not that you could have told from the face. He – she – could have given Dietrich points. The make-up's expert too.'

'If it's a man, I mean, *as* it's a man,' Cryer said, 'I certainly didn't cotton on when she spent hours here, last week, telling me about what research she'd do for Alex Hervey.' Bone was at the door with Foster, and Cryer, getting up to follow, diverted Jem's effort to come too, turning him towards Edwina.

'Corpses, male or female, definitely not on your breakfast menu this or any other morning, my son.'

Bone could not help remembering that young Jemmy had found a corpse a year ago. He hoped it was not to prove a family habit.

'Noel Prestbury was in something of a state about the article Hervey wrote on his place. You know it's called Prestbury too? They've had the house since the Reformation or something.' Cryer was accompanying them along the stone-flagged passage with its Kirghiz carpet. In a niche stood another carved wooden saint, with that Renaissance sway of the body. 'I agreed conditionally to let them do this house, provided they played up the security angle. Security – my God, bit of a joke now.'

'You didn't at all suspect it wasn't a girl?'

'A whole afternoon and she was sweet as pie, her hair over her face like at the party.' They were in the entrance hall now and could hear the search of the party rooms. 'She was businesslike, tweeds and silk shirt, cool. Only minimal come-on, but I fancied her all right. Reminded me of Archangel, bone structure or something. She was good-looking in that same rather unreal way. I didn't suspect, all the same. No, Robert, I'm not jealous of Archangel. I sell as much as he does, perhaps more, and he's said to me often enough that his looks mean the critics believe he *can't* be any good, the dumb blonde syndrome. As you can see, I've never had that trouble.' Cryer's face had always been more notorious for bone than for beauty. It had been intensely lived in: lined, hollow and pale.

People were getting up; as they climbed the stairs someone overhead called out, 'Not the fuzz? Not really?' and an unshaven face peered over the balustrade. Bone silently saluted. There was a sharp retreat into bedrooms.

33

In Cryer's room, the body lay on plastic sheeting, the dress decently tucked now round the knees. As the three came in, the crew stood back and looked at the body thoughtfully, much as though they were wrapping a somewhat bizarre present.

The face, now clearly seen with its own blond hair sleeked back, was fine-boned, smooth, the make-up still imparting a feminine air but the revealed ears and neck of masculine size. It was an arresting face, the proportions balanced, the mouth lightly sculptured, nose short and neat, skin smooth.

'Do you know him?'

Ken crouched to see the profile.

'No. It bloody *is* like Archangel, though. Wonder who the hell it is?' Ken stood up slowly, frowning, and drew back.

'You can't identify.'

'No.'

'Thank you.' Bone now regarded the enigma with increased interest. Impersonators as good as this one had been must be reasonably rare. A case one didn't come across every day. He said "I'll be down later,' moving Cryer towards the door. 'You said he, she, came with Tansley-Ferrars.'

'Lives in Biddenden. Woodlings.'

'"Would—"?'

'House name. Woodlings.'

'Thank you.'

Cryer, with a glance back over his shoulder, went quickly out. He was hugging his arms to himself again.

Ferdy Foster drew Bone to the window-seat, while the team deftly covered their prize, put it on the stretcher and wheeled it from the room. Ferdy peered over his spectacles at the garden hazed in bright mist that promised hot sun later.

'Thought you'd like to know straight away all I can say now about the wounds.'

'Wounds. Plural.'

'Not only plural but from different directions.'

Bone shaped his lips to a silent whistle and stared at the window-curtain. With part of his mind he took in that it was sprigged with the same wool-embroidered flowers of blue and white as the bedspread, to which the victim had so inconsiderately added red. At the same time he visualized the baroque scenario of a murderer dodging round the bed for a second go; anxious to make sure, or just liked the feeling? Ferdy observed his face with satisfaction and moved to the door.

'Of course, it appears that the second time he was shot he'd been dead for at least a short while.'

Bone caught up with Ferdy as he pattered down the stairs humming one of his little tunes, a man looking forward to his work. Ferdy's habit of theatrical exit-lines was one Bone knew well, also his great tendency on the phone to hang up on a punch-line with the effect of an exclamation mark.

'Is that all you can say?'

'Certainly.' Ferdy's Indian-ink eyes looked surprised over the half-lenses. 'You can't expect, Robert, that I could say any more as yet.'

He followed his day's work out of the side door. Bone thought Ferdy had said quite enough, all things considered. How could it be possible that Bone, going peacefully to bed last night after sharing a Chinese takeaway with his daughter Charlotte, was now not so many hours later involved with an unidentified corpse that had been carefully shot twice and which was dressed as a woman?

Not to mention that it had happened at a party whose guest list was composed for the most part of those people with whom Bone was least accustomed to dealing, most of whom had disappeared into the wide blue yonder, some yonder than others, like Archangel taking in Wembley on his way to New York, and all of them would have to be interviewed. He found, and fed himself, another peppermint tablet.

Locker came into the hall to tell him at what hour Ferdy expected to be ready for the post mortem.

'That gives time for one of us to go and see Tansley-Ferrars. I'll take Sergeant Shay and leave all the rest of the interviewing here to you, Steve, and don't say "Big Deal". After the post mortem we'll forgather at Saxhurst; they're setting up an incident room there.'

'Citizens' Advice Bureau,' Locker said grimly.

'I doubt it; they hadn't enough power plugs last time. But don't look a gift horse in the mouth.'

'Don't like its teeth, sir. Right, see you there.'

Breakfast for overnight waifs was in the small brown room which the house-agent had called the breakfast room, seldom used by Ken. Several people came or stumbled down the two steps and found places at the table. Edwina, now with a gold gauze scarf as a tie, looked in to assure everyone's comfort.

Five people raised their eyes as she entered, if not their heads. The guitarist with blond ringlets and lined face, an awesome mixture of Shirley Temple and Rip Van Winkle, shut his eyes again at once. Edwina did not take this personally. He had done the traditional thing and come off hard drugs with some publicity and, by medical reckoning, in the nick of time, but he had forgotten to come off alcohol and was particularly deep-etched this morning; a face more lilac than white, with toning darker lavender shadows around the eyes. A journalist friend of Edwina's, working on a series about rock stars who had rejected drugs (*Heroes against Heroin*) had decided to leave out Roy Ray, since he was a bad advertisement for anything short of death. Roy was now being ministered to by his girlfriend Tanya, black and sinuous, enviably untouched by the hangover of the others, even by the vulture wings of Roy's. She wore a chiffon number in orange, as fresh as the juice she drank now. She was getting Roy to drink Perrier. He was in black leather trousers that only he could have got into, that would take a shoehorn and Tanya to get him out of, and a silk shirt ripped and stained, very likely on purpose. He moaned because, opening his eyes again, he saw Tanya eating a sausage in her fingers. He had lost his dark glasses, broken last night, Tanya said.

'Has Ken a spare pair? Someone in the crowd shoved Roy and knocked them off his face.'

'Likely the murderer,' Roy husked.

The other couple mirrored them in reverse. The girl, white, wore a boned black satin dress with frills from hip to thigh, less fetching by daylight than it had seemed the night before. This extended to her, the tumble of crimped yellow hair in need of a dye job as the roots matched her dress. She shuddered from the scrambled eggs her partner was eating. He, a large silent black, was a brilliant drummer whom Ken had used alongside Si Worth on tours. Perfectly happy to eat everything on the table, he cast sympathetic glances at Roy now and then.

Sutton Somerton was the odd one out, drinking coffee avidly and twitching. His height made him look awkward even when sitting down, as though nothing that had been made would accommodate his legs, and he looked resentful of this. He had a long, melancholy face, the eyes large and hooded, the chin obstinate. He stared with indiscriminate detestation at the others.

'Did anyone know this Alix?' Tanya asked. 'Anyone see anything strange?'

Edwina thought this could apply to any of them except the drummer, and she was sorry for the nice policeman. Tanya went on, 'You don't look for this sort of thing in the English countryside. Okay in New York, right, but out here it's kind of a shock.'

'I don't see why you should think nothing ever happens here,' the other girl said. Edwina remembered Mrs Bennett's indignation that Mr Darcy should suppose there was no scandal in the English countryside. Don't disparage the boondocks.

'Can I get anything else for anyone?' she asked. 'Dark glasses for Roy, yes. Did everyone sleep all right – considering?' The consideration being a murder they had presumably not been aware of. How had Macbeth's guests slept during Duncan's murder? She remembered *that* night had been stormy, and after the banquet there were no doubt hangovers as bad as Roy's.

'Oh yes, slept fine.'

'Thanks, Edwina. We couldn't have been more comfortable.'

Roy, his eyes once again shut, his head no doubt twanging in every fibre as plangently as his Stratocaster, opened his mouth and after an appreciable struggle spoke.

'Not a hell of a lot of chance to get any sleep in. The party dies one minute, the next there's police roarin' through the place asking questions.'

The white girl, whose name Edwina could not recall, said, 'I hate the police,' as though she'd just been offered them for breakfast.

'I hope they didn't upset anyone too much. Inspector Locker is a really nice man.'

'They're all pigs.' Remembering her name now, Edwina thought 'Oriane' wasted on her.

Edwina held her peace. Robert Bone could hardly appear porcine even to the most prejudiced eye.

'They only doing they work,' said the drummer, and crunched toast.

'They do nothing but ask stupid questions,' snapped Oriane.

Ask a stupid girl a stupid question, get a stupid answer, thought Edwina. She said, 'Routine's a bore, whatever it's about. Who will be wanting lunch? You'd best not travel yet, Roy.'

'Have to be in London by one. Meeting someone. Tanya'll drive.'

'If anyone would like to stay, tell me now so I can warn the kitchen; I'm going shopping in Tenterden and I shan't be back in time.'

Somerton from the end of the table spoke for the first time. 'I'd like a lift. If you don't mind.'

Of course. He'd been ditched by the girl he came with, who'd zoomed off in her car without him. A row must account for his distracted agitation, that and the humiliation of being stranded. He had an invalid wife, which was a shame, and Edwina felt it was awkward not to be more sorry for him. His nervy hostility was so far from amiable.

'Of course,' she said warmly. 'Ready in half an hour.'

Although she had still five minutes of the half hour in hand, she found Somerton fretting on the gravel in front of the Manor. Ken, casting her a glance of thanksgiving, had been in conversation with him. She saw how much his civility was under strain. The men stood by the raised basin of the pond in the centre of the drive's sweep, near the stone putti clasping each other in petrified affection at one side. It was possibly a last night's guest who had put a cigarette between the parted lips of one cherub, giving him an air of infant dissipation as he leant over his reflection in the pool, decidedly like Dylan Thomas contemplating a bath.

Somerton darted forward as he saw Edwina, with no more than perfunctory thanks and farewell to Ken. She thought, here's someone who didn't have a good party, and she opened the door of the estate car. He jack-knifed in. Ken waved to her, his face creasing into an affectionate smile, and turned, as she circled to the driver's side, towards the house; whence issued a Dance of Death onto the gravel, woven by the emerging Roy Ray, in Ken's spare dark glasses, one hand on Tanya's shoulder, the other raised against the mild sun; following him the wincing Oriane, daylight giving her black satin frills a final touch of silliness; her head dropped, her tights were laddered, she tottered on little heels, a trashed dolly.

Somerton put the seat back with a jolt. Edwina fastened her seat belt, thinking *height, width, we all have our problems*. She set off, waiting a second at the gates, smiling at the eye of the TV for Mel to spring the gates for her. She tried at first to make pleasant conversation, avoiding mention of Somerton's errant girl-friend and the reason he needed a lift home. Enquiries about his wife went down badly. She felt growing sympathy for the girl-friend. She wondered, falling silent, whether his wife knew of the girl-friend, how Somerton coped with a bedridden wife who could not accompany him anywhere. She couldn't remember hearing what was wrong with Mrs Somerton. Was it M.S.? Somerton had always, in Ken's phrase, been a moody bugger all through their acquaintance over the renovation and alteration of the barn into a studio. There had been trouble with

41

the builder, Ken having to act as mediator when he should have been spared just that. Somerton was a brilliant architect, all right, simply rather bad at being a *person*.

They passed, now, a house where builders were at work on the roof, the noticeboard outside giving the firm's name. Somerton ducked to see, and remarked with satisfaction, '*They're* no good. Roof will be bound to leak before the year's out.' She saw his glare and thought he was hexing the men. A wonder they didn't keel off the ladders as the car went by.

He directed her to a house in the main street in Tenterden. To the left, the verge ran down in a bank towards the wide pavement, where people sauntered past elegant houses, many now converted to offices, restaurants and crafty little shops, no longer inhabited solely by the families who had once been able to live there. Somerton had a house opposite, beyond a long front garden, removed from the street's tree-lined genteel hurly-burly by a flowery length. Edwina was fleetingly surprised that he didn't live in a house of his own design, a showpiece for his talents, as did many architects. Perhaps he didn't like even his own work.

'Just here, by the black Volvo, my car. There. Thank you *so* much.' His effusiveness felt like an expression of his hostility, politeness used as an insult. He managed a smile, and backed out of the car. She expected him to go through the garden gate but he stood there, by his car, the smile still pinned across his face.

42

On an impulse, she said, putting her head out, 'Can I do any shopping for your wife?'

The smile distorted. He bent down, always with further to go than most people, so that one expected him to splay his legs like a giraffe, and said in at the window, '*How* kind. Oh, no thank you. All that is taken care of, quite taken care of. It's charming of you. No, thank you.' He withdrew, nearly catching the top of his head, and, still standing there behind his car, waved her resolutely away.

She let in the clutch and drove off to park by the bookshop. She had to collect Ken's watch from the jeweller's by the church, and get marshmallows for Jem, pâté from the deli . . . half an hour later, when she drove home, the black Volvo had gone. Perhaps he did all the shopping. She felt more sorry for him, and therefore more comfortable about him, and a good deal more able to be sorry for him out of his presence.

The newspapers lay beside her where he had sat. Tomorrow would *The Times* have a front-page paragraph, *The Star* take half a page to shout *Death at Cryer Mansion*? If anyone slipped into *Cryer in Transvestite Killing*, could Ken sue?

Bone's driver found Woodlings without trouble: a small, rather hunchbacked house with thatch so elaborate it should almost be finished with bows at either end, and a species of cross-stitch in front. Set back from the uneven stone pavement, in the older part of the village, it had a path at the side past the front door, with a glimpse beyond of overgrown

43

garden shadowed by trees. A small house to encompass a hyphenated name, thought Bone, as Sergeant Shay's car stopped behind his and they got out.

The knocker on the sturdy oak door was a dolphin in brass, and Bone tapped with it just as the church clock, alarmingly near, struck seven. It occurred to Bone that Jay Tansley-Ferrars might well, after a party, be far from awake and unwilling to be woken.

Something was awake. A maddening, tinny bark advanced to settle behind the front door and give of its best. Some minutes of monotonous barking later, as Bone was about to knock yet again despite an unworthy urge to kick the foot of the door at the height of the bark's source, a bolt was shot back inside. The door opened, and an ankle-threatening little dog burst out as though from a gun, ignored Bone and Shay entirely, careered to the gate, yapped defiance at the morning street through the lower bars, turned, and belted back down the side of the house to the garden, where he fell so silent so immediately that Bone imagined some Black Hole of the canine universe.

'I paid the milk yesterday,' said Jay Tansley-Ferrars, looking Bone and Shay up and down with a distaste more focused than his dog's. Striped pyjamas marginally too big for him gave him a vulnerable air at odds with the inimical frown. There was a plume of grey in the hair swept off the high forehead engraved with lines; the eyebrows rose in a wistful curve over large, dark eyes, the eyes of a wounded Bambi full of mistrust. The door was closing when the eyes took in Bone's warrant card. Tansley-Ferrars blinked and stayed his hand.

'Mr Jay Tansley-Ferrars? Can I have a word with you, please?'

The door slowly opened. 'My God. It's come at last. What's my little brother done now?'

Bone registered this for future reference. 'It's about Ken Cryer's party. There was an incident we are having to investigate.'

Tansley-Ferrars stood back to let them pass him and, shutting the door, led the way down a narrow hall smelling of damp and carpeted in matting so frayed that Bone at once caught his foot and barely saved himself from pushing his host into the dark room they entered. Used to taking in scenes at a glance, he saw through the width of window that trees formed a semi-circle round a terrace where wrought-iron chairs lurked; one of these lay on its back with twisted legs drunkenly in the air. The dog was nowhere visible.

'An incident covers quite an area doesn't it? One sees the police treating the Day of Judgement as an incident. God the Father will be questioned quite severely over *that* little affair. Do sit.'

The sofa, comfortable in coral wool, faced the garden and was in front of a huge tapestry where huntsmen were doing unpleasant things to various animals. As Bone sat, he felt the atmosphere curiously closed in after the freshness of the early morning outside. It was not that the room itself was stuffy, but that here the day had not begun. Tansley-Ferrars was lighting a cigarette after a mute offer of his case, which he kept behind the cushion of the chair he had taken. Perhaps he didn't trust the dog not to smoke.

'What's happened then?' He drew smoke, put back his head and exhaled it. 'Did that drunk murder someone after all?'

'Drunk, sir?'

He gestured impatiently, scrawling smoke on the air. 'The bloke who hit . . . oh, there were various little lost tempers but his was the one most likely to succeed.'

'You brought a guest with you, I understand.'

'Mm. We had dinner here and went on. Do I tell you who she is or do you already know or do I tell you anyway?'

'You tell me anyway.'

The sad eyes checked to see if this was a joke, took in Bone's impassivity and looked away. The face all at once crumpled and Tansley-Ferrars yawned comprehensively. He wiped his eyes on his sleeve and said, 'Alix Hamilton, this gorgeous girl from London, and Magnus Haywood, who lives here, had dinner; but he was ill and didn't come on with us to Ken's.'

'Was Alix Hamilton to come back here?'

The dark eyes blinked surprise. 'Here? Oh no, she said I had only to take her there, and once there she would shift for herself.' This phrase conjured the image of a scaffold in Bone's mind but he had no time to trace it. 'Alix is *not* a girl to need her hand held. Though the party was a wee bit fraught for her because who should she see first thing but her boss's wife? We did some

46

hide-and-seek, quite fun.' He seemed to enjoy this in retrospect.

'Was there a reason why Alix Hamilton should need to avoid her boss's wife?'

'Oh—' the cigarette waved airily – 'the research assistant being a glamorous chick and the wife . . . the usual story. Alix thought Lamia Hervey was giving her the evil eye, and didn't wish to meet. That's all. Should there be more?' Bone opened his note book and unfolded the guest list. As he had thought, no Lamia Hervey.

'The incident involved Alix Hamilton.' Bone had been doing his sums: Alix Hamilton, Alexander Hervey. Alix avoiding Hervey's wife. 'Surely meeting the wife is no great deal even these days for a research assistant however glamorous.'

Jay Tansley-Ferrars was now covertly amused. The mouth's corners were twitching. He said, 'Oh, I don't know. Lamia was not looking *at all* cosy.'

'Do you know Lamia Hervey?'

'Have met. Don't *know*. But how did this "incident" involve Alix?'

'Alix is dead.'

Tansley-Ferrars dropped his cigarette. His face showed pure shock. It was a full second before he panic-searched for the cigarette, burnt his fingers, picked it up and, giving his fingers a distracted perfunctory lick, brushed ash from his legs, staring at Bone.

'So perhaps you would confirm some information for us?'

'Dead! I mean – Christ – what happened?'

47

'At the moment I can tell you very little.'

'Well . . . I suppose you've examined . . . I suppose you *know*.'

'Who was he, Mr Tansley-Ferrars?'

'Alex Hervey. I believe he'd been doing it for years, cross-dressing. Brilliant as a woman, became a different person. He's not gay. I mean he didn't take it on further . . . I mean, he's not a close friend but I know he got a kick out of the female role and I've done this before, sort of vouched for Alix Hamilton and taken her out, say four or five times. When he asked.'

'As a joke.'

'Yes, that's exactly it. A joke of a sort. Jesus, though. You see how he had to avoid Lamia. He was sure she'd unveil him if he got close enough. I'm not certain she didn't spot him, because she did seem to pursue a bit; but perhaps that was just the jealousy, wanting to confront her husband's little bit on the side. But I was enjoying the party so I did let Alex shift for himself.'

This time Bone traced the quotation: Sir Thomas More going up to the scaffold, accepting help and saying: *on the way down I can shift for myself*, or was it *you may leave me to shift for myself* . . .

'Did it happen then? Did *she* do it? In the middle of eveything, us all partying and that? And he . . . where was he?'

Bone did not reply. 'What I must ask you to do,' he said, 'is to tell Sergeant Shay all you can remember about the party; such as whom you talked to, anything you noticed, people's behaviour.'

'God, I can't remember.' Tansley-Ferrars was

still shaken. 'Poor Alex. Do I have to do all that? I don't remember any kind of detail. I really can't.'

'You could come to Saxhurst later in the day; to the station,' Bone offered blandly.

'How very inviting. If I don't do either, do I get arrested?'

'Is there any reason for not doing either?'

Tansley-Ferrars stubbed out his cigarette. 'God, no, except that it's impossible to remember. It's early morning. I've had about three hours' sleep.'

Lucky old you, thought Bone. He said, ruthless, 'It will be fresh in your mind.' He stood up. Tansley-Ferrars dragged himself to his feet and stretched. Sergeant Shay was examining a small hanging corner cabinet that a little, deep window shed light on. It contained model soldiers, a score or so.

'Do you collect, sir?' he asked.

'Would if I could. Do you *know* about them?' His tone suggested the extreme unlikelihood, but Sergeant Shay refused offence.

'Only enough to know there's some very old ones there, sir. My grandfather had a few of them from when he was a boy, and they sold for more than he expected.'

Tansley-Ferrars said, 'Here,' and led the way across the hall passage to what might have been the dining room. It was dominated by a big map-table and on the walls hung battle pictures, prints mostly, of engravings or of paintings. He pulled out a cabinet drawer. 'Blenheim, Malplaquet, Oudenarde,' he said. 'The one on the table's Waterloo.' He was impatient. 'That's what I do. I

49

know about battles. Waterloo's a cliché, but I had a bunch of schoolchildren yesterday on one of their pathetic little projects. I use overlays to give the state of the battle at different stages. I read them Georgette Heyer's account of the battle, much the best.'

'I wish I'd time,' Bone said, interested.

'But you haven't.' He shut the drawer dismissively. 'A busy man with a job to do.'

A high keening started up somewhere, a wronged and tragic cry like a faulty chainsaw. Tansley-Ferrars led the way to the front door. The dog came past them before it was well open, a dark smear on the wall showing his habitual passage. He vanished into the depths of the house and there was a sound of violent lapping.

'Thank you, Mr Tansley-Ferrars,' said Bone, and left him to Sergeant Shay.

CHAPTER FOUR

His next task was to deal with Mrs Alexander
Hervey. Standing in the street, he again consulted
Edwina's guest list, and he got his ideas together on
his way back to Saxhurst.

Locker reported, on the phone from the Manor,
'Getting on nicely, sir. Only one real item. A
waiter, one of the Indonesian kitchen staff, thinks a
woman guest had a small gun in her bag. He saw her
drop it in the crush, and picked it up before she did,
and she was angry. He felt the weight and shape.
She was, he says, a Northern woman. He hasn't
much English, except about food.'

'A Northern woman.'

'Pak Sim interpreted. Cryer's cook, their boss.
They're most of them his relations.'

'He can't do better than "Northern".'

'No, sir. And I've been thinking: to an Indonesian, he might not think about Scotland, or Scandi-
navian, like we would, and how would he know a
Scots accent? Northern would mean *his* northern.'

'We could be looking for a Chinese woman.'

'Miss Marsh says one guest was slightly Chinese.
She didn't know her, she came with one of the men.
She and Cryer've been trying to work out which it
was. I don't quite make out how Oriental she looks
but I gather the general effect is a bit stunning.'

'Hardly exact, "stunning"?'

'Rum do, this drag thing. Cryer's quite narked at not having spotted it.'

'Tansley-Ferrars says Hervey was brilliant as a woman.'

'*Hervey*, sir?'

'I'm ninety per cent certain.'

There was silence on the other end of the line, and Bone smiled at the phone. 'But we're not giving out on this. Officially, for the press, it's still a woman. And Tansley-Ferrars had something else to say. He saw Lamia Hervey at the party and she's not on the guest list. No one else seems to have recognized her but the victim. Apparently Lamia Hervey had a grudge against her husband's girl-friend and was pursuing her at the party.'

'Her husband's girl-friend?'

'Alix Hamilton. I'm off to London for a word with Mrs Hervey, and I'll take Pat Fredricks. See you.'

He rang off, put through a request for a car and WDC Fredricks to be available at Tunbridge Wells for the London visit, and went over what had been so far collected. The most interesting was the discovery that someone, in rubber-soled shoes, had stood about in Ken Cryer's bathroom, had used the loo but not the flush, and had left a thumb-print under the seat. On the polished cork tiles, his shifting feet had left their marks, close to the door, so that he must have stood listening. The thumb print had come through on the HOLMES computer: one Mick Parsons, form for breaking and entering, petty theft, who, yes, had been at the party, having come with Gwyn Griffiths, Ken's video director. They had put out word for him and were making enquiries of Griffiths and Cryer about him.

Bone called Chelsea to say he would be on their patch, collected a present-status print-out, and set off for Tunbridge Wells after a final word with the incident room's office manager.

On the drive, he would have liked to have had Steve along to talk things out with. Did Lamia Hervey know of her husband's cross-dressing? Was she actually after her husband or the 'girl-friend'? If she knew of the impersonation, was she for it or against it? Her 'pursuit' of Alix Hamilton suggested she did not know. She must have tried to be unobtrusive about it, for the party was not so vast that she could not, surely, have encountered 'Alix' had she tried.

Suppose Hervey were killed by the thief of the monstrance. Who then put him in the bed? If the thief were the Brown Brother who threatened Cryer, he might well be a nutter, but to tidy the supposed woman into Cryer's bed . . . and Ferdy Foster would be able to say how likely that was. In Bone's mind lay the heavy shadow of the post mortem.

To put the body in the bed was hardly more kinky than anything else in this case. Yet suppose he-she had been in the bed already, waiting for an assignation or a surprise meeting, half-hidden by the curtains, then making a sound, speaking, alarming the intruder who then took the gun . . .

How had she got into the locked room before

the intruder, the thief who had unlocked door and drawer? Had Parsons opened both and then fled for the bathroom when she came . . .

Jay Tansley-Ferrars' reaction to the news of death had rung true, and so far he totally lacked motive. Unless, in a scenario springing partheno-genetically in Bone's imagination, he resented Hervey's not being gay, and resented it to the point of murder.

If the monstrance were the only thing taken, it pointed to the Brown Brother, whoever *he* was; in that case, why was the bedside drawer forced?

Had the thief of the monstrance killed Hervey in mistake for Cryer? That went too far from sense. Alex Hervey hadn't even been looking like a man.

The most likely thing was that Hervey had got into the bed to wait for someone, most likely a man. He had taken advantage of the sprung lock, scared the thief into the bathroom, and – had the thief opened the drawer to make a gun available for a killer?

Bone reached headquarters, had a word with his chief, found WDC Fredricks ready, and gave her the print-out to read as they went. Plain-clothes with her meant just that; something in brown cotton with a loose jacket, not memorable, but it suited her colouring. She had a strong, bony, plain face and was admirably efficient.

He fell asleep in the car, awkwardly, in discomfort but ineluctably, and woke as they were coming across the Albert Bridge. He was cramped, dazed, embarrassed. Fredricks took his sleeping for granted and he was relieved that she did not tactfully, smilingly, make allowance for him. One day, he thought, I shall achieve an Olympian detachment about these things, the right damn-you attitude so many superior officers display.

He was quite unaware that Pat Fredricks admired the calm way he woke without excuse and was at once looking around, taking in where they were.

The driver found the street through the one-way system, and double-parked to let them off in Cheyne Row outside the Queen Anne house over-shadowed by a vast Tree of Heaven. He drove away to park, while they climbed green and grimy steps. People were going in to Mass at St Thomas the Redeemer on the corner. An elderly woman passed, putting black lace on her grey coiffure with gloved hands and an air of conscious virtue. But don't judge, he thought. What do I know about spiritual pride, except how easy it is to commit? Fredricks turned towards the door, which was opening.

The woman was in a white brocade housecoat, her almond-shaped eyes dark and anxious, going from him to Fredricks, her hair in black torrents over her shoulders, a light golden tan and no make-up, but dark circles round the eyes. She stared at his warrant card and began to breathe deep as if alarmed, and backed out of their way.

They followed her into the front room. He had an impression of cream and green, a large Chinese carpet, a green brocade sofa and chairs. Over the mantel, a painting of a temple and landscape in dingy oils looked out of place. Magazines littered the floor, a D-J on the radio assured them that the next track was the one they'd all asked for.

Mrs Hervey turned off the radio and sank on the sofa as though her legs had failed. She did not seem able to speak, looking, still, from one to the other as if she could not decide which part of the nightmare was worse, or how to wake up.

Bone broke the news, wondering if in fact it was news at all. 'I'm very sorry to have to tell you, Mrs Hervey, that we have reason to believe that your husband Alexander Hervey has been involved in a fatal incident.'

'Fatal?' she said. The eyes fixed on him, dark and glazed. 'How could he be? What's he done?'

'It seems he was shot.' (And perhaps by you? he wondered.) The phrases, seems to have been, reason to believe, the professional protection, irritated him.

'He? What do you mean? You don't mean he's killed himself?'

'It does not appear like that.' Nobody shoots himself under the left arm and clears the gun away.

'*When* did this happen? *Who* shot him?' If her astonishment and horror were an act, she was in line for an Oscar.

'It happened at Ken Cryer's, last night or early this morning.'

'But he wasn't there. He told me he wasn't going.'

And in a sense that was the truth. 'He did go, however. He was shot in Cryer's bedroom, in strange—'

Her face had contorted, her hands covered her

56

mouth and she broke out shrieking 'No!' the only distinct word emerging through the hooting laughter of hysteria.

Fredricks took hold of her, and with a mixture of coaxing and no-nonsense decisiveness got her partly calmed down. She sagged on Fredricks' arm and, shuddering, said, 'Could I have a drink? There's brandy on the kitchen table.'

Fredricks was depositing her on the sofa ready to get this, as her questioning glance indicated. Bone, however, with his inveterate curiosity, followed Mrs Hervey's gesture, through an archway hung with a heavy green-and-cream plush curtain, through a second room whose table and sideboard held a mixture of papers, magazines, letters, brandy bottles, clothes and dishes, through an open door into a small kitchen where used crockery stood on table and draining-boards and there were tights in the sink. A window gave onto a dark backyard, and from the sill a large black cat stared in at Bone resentfully. The defunct Alex Hervey, whatever his feelings for dresses, possibly had no liking for aprons. The cat half-rose and gave a soundless mew; Bone pushed the window up enough to let it come in, but it crouched, scowling. He put brandy from a near-empty bottle in a tumbler, the only clean glass he could find, and came back with it.

She drank, sat a moment evidently waiting for the effect, then gave a nod of thanks, and raised her head. In that movement of the head and look of the almond eyes he could see that she might be, in the right mood, the right light, and made up, beautiful.

'I don't understand how he was there,' she said, 'but he *must* have killed himself.'

'What makes you think that, Mrs Hervey?'

She put the black swathes of her hair back, behind her shoulders. He noticed, inappropriately, that she had bare feet, the toenails painted like little pink shells.

'Was it because of that woman?' She leant forward, intent.

'Woman, Mrs Hervey?'

Tapping the glass impatiently on her knee she said, 'Woman. His secretary. Assistant. Alix Hamilton. *That* woman.' He was about to put in something temporizing, out of habit, when she went on, 'He adored her. He was wrapped up in her. She lived at his flat.'

'At his flat?'

'He had to have a separate place to write in. He said. He said this place distracted him.'

Bone, thinking of the kitchen, saw the possible point.

'She lived there with him.' Bone, as was his habit, made the question a statement.

'Jane, a friend – someone I can really trust – her kitchen overlooks the mews. She saw that woman going in and out just as if she owned the place.'

'Surely that's natural to a research assistant?'

Fredricks was watching him thoughtfully. She must wonder why he didn't come out with it.

'The woman would leave first thing in the morning when Jane was getting breakfast. She'd phone me, and it was always when Alex had spent the night there.'

'There is something you have to know, Mrs Hervey. There was no such person as Alix Hamilton.'

'But—'

His voice overrode her. 'Your husband used to dress as a woman. As Alix Hamilton. He was dressed as Alix Hamilton when he was shot last night.'

The glass left her hand, the brandy made a sparkling arc and fell on Bone, on the sofa, Fredricks. She was on her feet, screaming, a series of one-pitch screams through a wide mouth. Her arms bent so that her fists crushed her breasts, and shook violently. The pink toenails dug into the carpet. The eyes stared. It was a Gorgon mask. All her beauty was gone, the corded neck and bared gums revolted him even while he felt pity.

Fredricks had vanished through the curtain. She came back with a tumbler of water that she flung sharply into the screaming face. Mrs Hervey gave a final indrawn screech and stopped, trembling and gasping.

'I can't have done,' she said, while Fredricks mopped her with a tea-towel. 'I can't have done, it's not possible—'

'Lamia Hervey, you are under arrest for the unlawful shooting of Alexander Hervey. I must warn you that you do not have to say anything, but anything you do say may be used in evidence.'

'I never would have shot Alex,' she said. 'It was that woman.' She took the tea-towel from Pat Fredricks and went on drying her neck, but her attention was elsewhere, on Bone as the recipient

59

of her inner story. 'She wouldn't speak at all, not a word. She sat there sneering at me. I told her I knew and that it had to stop, I don't know what I said but I told her. All she did was sneer. Sitting there. All her hair. But I could see the sneering. I did shoot her. What happened? Did Alex find her and kill himself? He didn't, he wouldn't. Not for her.'

'She was Alex, Mrs Hervey, dressed as a woman.'

'It couldn't be. It's not possible. I'd have known.'

Bone was silent. People saw what they wanted to see, what they expected. She had watched Alex during the evening, and nothing could prove better, more fatally, that he could transform his whole identity into Alix Hamilton.

A woman he knew had told him once, about her extremely good-looking husband, that he was such a narcissist, if he'd had an identical twin he would have been gay. Alex Hervey could *become* the person he loved.

He called his driver in. They shut up the house and locked the windows. The cat was discovered on the cooker-top eating from a pan. Fredricks and Lamia Hervey came down from the bedroom, Lamia dressed, Fredricks carrying a smart tapestry holdall. Lamia was in a white silk shirt, a dark brown slim skirt, dark brown tights and shoes. She had swept the mass of her hair back to be held by a wooden clasp at the back of her head, and she had put on make-up. Bone saw his driver look her over with appreciation, a faint swivel of the jaw that meant *tasty*. Bone, recognizing her looks and style as above the ordinary, found as usual that he was not stirred by them. Since his wife's death some curious chill had descended on his responses, and only quite recently he had found his emotions returning to life, tentatively. Yet he felt as a subject of a miracle might do, unwilling to trust his weight to a paralysed limb.

He rang Chelsea police, who conveyed congratulations on the arrest but were not falling over themselves with joy when he mentioned the cat. He thought of the RSPCA and, though Fredricks found the number, he had second thoughts, and tried to phone his friend Mrs Playfair in Saxhurst. When he could not get an answer he said to Fredricks, 'Never mind, I'll take it just the same.' Mrs Hervey sat in dreary composure while Fredricks found the cat basket; after an abortive effort by Bone, the driver, who had gloves, put the cat in and got the wire door shut before it could reverse. Accompanied by an atmosphere of brandy and an *obbligato* of low yowls, they went out to the car.

The journey gave him time for thought, but thought as such eluded him; his mind embarked on speculation, reminiscence, visualizing and daydream. Beyond Lamia Hervey, whose scent a little counteracted the persistent brandy, was WDC Fredricks' neat and noble profile. The cat mistrustfully warbled, strapped into the front seat, and turned about with a creaking of wicker.

Bone's mental processes went: *what about the monstrance?*

Mick Parsons.

Why did Alex Hervey get into the bed?

Post mortem.

Mick Parsons.

That last parents' meeting. Grizel Shaw is Cha's form-mistress. A strong face, very much alive.

The Brown Brother and the monstrance.

How are the teams getting on with that guest list?

Trace, Interview, Eliminate.

Grizel Shaw. Pale hair and extraordinary vivid eyes.

Lamia Hervey had telephoned a solicitor, who advized her to say nothing more unless in the presence of her legal representative. He could send someone from the practice down to Kent in the morning, or alert someone local. She was apathetic, wanted him to decide; with a slight impatience audible to Bone, he had said, 'Leave it to me, then. Someone will be there in the morning.'

One person's tragedy is someone else's nuisance.

Death threats to Ken Cryer.

'The cat's called Tombola,' Mrs Hervey said, almost drowsily, so that Bone wondered if she had managed to take anything else after the brandy. Would it be possible to slip something in her mouth undetected by Fredricks, while she was dressing? Unlikely; this was more likely the effect of the shock of death.

'It's Alex's cat, not mine. Will it be put down?'

'Oh no. I know a woman who'll look after it.'

'Oh.'

The driver threaded among the South London streets. Bone wondered at the people living in this dingy, crowded world, perhaps born here, living with no space around. Animals killed when their space was invaded.

Mick Parsons lives in such a world.

Have they got hold of him yet?

Did he hear shots? Run out past the body in the bed?

Did he shoot?

What did he want with the monstrance? Had he a sale ready?

I doubt if he is deeply religious.

'Mrs Hervey; it's not to do with the case as far as you are concerned, or so I believe, but did you notice an ornament on the carved chest in that bedroom?'

'No. There wasn't anything on the chest. I mean there were candlesticks. Do you mean candlesticks?'

'No.'

'Am I supposed to have stolen something as well?' The voice was indifferent. There was no energy for indignation.

'No,' he said, adding with his ingrained caution, 'Not that I know of.'

'I didn't.'

What could she be thinking about, sitting there? Could she realize she had shot her husband and not lose her mind? What is she going through?

The face, more Chinese with the hair back, looked calm and empty. He hoped she was as numb as she appeared.

After the car smash that killed his wife and the baby, he had for a good while been incredulous of its having happened. Petra would at any moment, surely, of course, walk into the ward, come towards him with her reserved, slighly crooked smile. When they took him to see Charlotte in intensive care, he caught himself wondering, all but asking, if her mother had been in to see her.

Mrs Hervey turned towards him. 'If you want to know more about Alex,' she said with a vague social smile, 'his cousin probably knows him best. Mark Serafin. You know, the singer Archangel.'

'Thank you,' he said.

'He was at the party.'

'Yes.'

She sat staring at the passing streets.

The car took a roundabout at slightly too high a speed. The three in the back swung like a blues trio. Tombola lurched in his basket and spat.

'Sorry, mate,' the driver said *sotto voce*, then, belatedly, 'Sorry, sir!'

Got his priorities right, Bone thought. *Well, Archangel. Of course he knew Alex-Alix, and Ken said of the body 'It bloody is like Archangel.'*

'She talked to him,' Mrs Hervey said, 'the woman. She and Mark were laughing, and they danced together.'

It did not surprise him that Mrs Hervey was not thinking of 'the woman' as her husband. He didn't blame her. Who could blame her?

A slight sound made him turn his head. She sat quite still, with tears running down her beautiful face and falling on her blouse or running down her neck. Fredricks produced a tissue and put it in her hand. She mopped her face and neck absently, and went on crying in complete silence. Bone delivered Mrs Hervey, dictated a report, phoned Steve

Locker at Saxhurst to say he was coming after the post mortem, and was there anything?

'The team allocated to Mark Serafin can't get in touch, sir. Seems he always goes to ground before a concert. They're still trying. If you were to lean on somebody? And Prestbury's been bloody-minded; his words were, "I am not getting out of bed for any damn fool sergeant. I'll speak to the officer in charge of the case." I would say being a J.P. makes him think he's J.C.'

'We might fit him into the timetable, Steve.'

'Right, sir. I'll tell the action allocator. And you, sir?'

'I've brought her back with me.'

'Really, sir? She?'

'It doesn't answer all our questions.'

Quite how many there were, Bone would not know until after the post mortem.

Meanwhile, because he was still reeking of brandy in a way that made his colleagues turn heads to stare, raise eyebrows and, if they had the rank to do it, comment, he went home to change; he got through to Emily Playfair at Saxhurst, who said cordially that he was to bring Tombola along at any time.

Tombola heaved to and fro as he was carried up the stairs to Bone's big flat on the top floors of the house. Probably he could smell Ziggy, Charlotte's cat. Ziggy was not about, however, as Bone took the basket into the kitchen. He was getting out a tin of catfood when he heard sounds overhead and became completely still. Ziggy could be noisy, but he did not make footsteps.

He strode out, and Grizel Shaw came running down the stairs, smiling, so much at home that he imagined he was dreaming it, or had managed some time-slip into an imagined event, a delightful scenario he didn't even know he had wanted written.

CHAPTER FIVE

'I've not broken in,' she called. 'Cha was not too well, with this tummy bug that's going about, and I brought her home. She's been sick a couple of times and she's much better now.'

She stood on the stairs. He found that he was gazing with his mouth ajar, and closed it.

'Cha said you'd not be in,' the Scots voice went on, 'so I thought she should not be alone . . . you look as much astonished as though I were indeed a burglar. Is it my teeshirt?'

Bone made another effort to remedy his expression. 'I can cope with burglars, I hope.' He took in what she was wearing, now that she posed with a hand on the banisters. He was not unwilling to observe. The teeshirt, striped in black and white, lent itself pleasantly to the lines of her body, and the gamine look was increased by baggy black trousers with a high waist. Bone reflected with gratitude that, since his years at school, teachers had become less conventional in their attire. He remembered the awesome Miss Mallett, Cha's headmistress, and admired her liberal attitude to her staff's appearance.

'I think you've left out the bag marked "Swag", haven't you?'

'On the other hand, I *have* got a flat cap.'

He believed her. He said, 'I'll just run up and see Cha. I reek of brandy, I'm afraid. It's a shame I hadn't the benefit of it, but it was somebody else's drink that was thrown about. I came home to change. I'm most grateful to you, looking after Cha. It must have put you out. Normally there's the housekeeper . . .'

'It didn't put me out at all. There's so many away with this tummy thing, and half the rest out on the trip to the Science Museum. There're plenty of staff to mind the shop.'

Cha's rebuilt leg would still not take long standing and walking periods, or long journeys without a stop. Mrs Shaw came down the stairs and paused; she conveyed by a small mime the impact of his suit's brandy, and they laughed. It was true, however dated or coy it sounded, Bone saw: eyes do sparkle.

A feeble cry of 'Daddy!' sent Bone up the stairs. As he came into Charlotte's room he heard from the kitchen a chink of cups, an extraordinarily comfortable sound, conjuring images of home, of his wife making a meal ready while he ran upstairs to see the children.

His one child was wan but cheerful. 'I've been ree-*voltingly* sick and I feel tons better. What's the funny smell?'

'Stale brandy. Nasty, isn't it? Someone spilt it on me. Sorry, I'll change in a moment.' He took off the jacket, which was the worst, and threw it onto the landing. 'Now, are you really all right, pet?'

'Yes. We couldn't find the magnesia tablets,

though. Are we out of them? Mrs Shaw went out and got me something from the chemist that was marvellous. She's great; she's so kind.'

'A nice woman. Ah, that's where Ziggy's got to.' He was in the curve of Charlotte's knees, a grey-marbled crescent of fur on the duvet. 'He hasn't any objection to your being home, m'm? Oh, and keep him up here just now, would you? I've a cat in a basket in the kitchen, on his way to Emily Playfair's. She kindly says she'll board him.'

'What's he like? Is he a stray?'

'He's large and black and, naturally, very cross. His owner's died and he's homeless.'

'Poor thing.' Charlotte's face, thin and cream-coloured on the pillow, was uncomfortably reminiscent of her state after the crash. However, nothing else was the same. Between her health, Grizel Shaw's presence, his reeking suit, and the need to get to the post mortem, he was for a moment dazed.

'I've got to go. You'll be all right now.'

'Sure,' she said valiantly. 'No problem. Much much better.'

He put the bottle of tablets on her bed-table. 'Bit late – I had these; started the morning with the gripes. Everyone's got it, you're in very good company along with Jem Cryer.' He went out to his room, picking up the jacket on the way.

'You've been to Ken Cryer's?' she called.

'Yes. There was an incident there.'

'He's all right – Ken Cryer?'

'All right, and doubtless good for dozens more albums.'

69

'Was he as gorgeous as ever?'

'Gorgeous?' He didn't want to make fun of her. 'That's not the precise word, chum. At four in the morning he looked suitably haggard, decayed and so on.'

'That's all just his charm.' She did not sound ill now.

'Do you know who'd been at the party too? Though he'd gone before I came.'

'Who? Who?'

'Archangel.'

'Oh no. Oh *Daddy* why did he have to go before you saw him?'

'It seems he wanted to get some sleep before tonight's Wembley.'

'I wished I could have gone to that. And he was there not all that far away. Oh just imagine him being at Ken Cryer's. Two of them in the same room. It must have been sizzling with sex.'

These observations were of a recent kind with Cha, and he had not found a mode of responding to them. He said, 'Probably.'

'They made a single together last year and it came in at five and went to number one.'

'Really?' Bone's simulated interest made her laugh.

'You're hopeless. I bet you don't even know what it was.'

Bone had an excellent memory for Cha's interests. He said, '*What it Takes*. This suit's for the cleaners. It'll have to wait until Mrs Ames gets back.'

'I can take it tomorrow.'

'We'll see. You mayn't be up to traipsing about.'

'I'm going to school. You don't think I'd miss the last day and break-up. The sixth form's doing a take-off of the staff. And then I'm going to Grue's for the day.'

He went in again briefly to kiss her. 'Well, Grue will take care of you. Sure you're really better?'

'Fuss-pot.'

Since he felt reasonably well in the stomach himself, he believed her, and ran downstairs to where Grizel Shaw was pouring tea in the kitchen. She looked up as he arrived.

'Better keep the door shut, I've opened the cat basket.' She had put a saucer of catfood down in front of the basket, and Tombola had made tentative inroads upon it but was again invisible.

'He's very hungry, poor creature, but not easy in his mind.'

'I don't think he's been fed this morning. He was stealing from a pan.'

'That doesn't mean a thing. Cats eat where they find food.' She sat opposite Bone at the small round table. He put milk in his tea and drank.

'I was thirsty.'

'Cha said you preferred tea to coffee.' Her eyes, friendly over the rim of the mug, took in his appearance. 'Is it a tiring case that you're on?'

'Do I look battered? I'd a touch of this tummy bug in the night and the call came at four.'

'Pause while I don't make the quotation about the policeman's lot.' She refilled his cup.

Bone smiled; and Grizel Shaw reflected that his face, like Charlotte's, was totally transformed by this smile. Normally he was given to a sardonic tightening of the mouth, which she had described as a touch of the Charlton Hestons. This was different.

'I must go,' he said, but didn't move.

'Look, Charlotte should have a fairly plain diet for a couple of days – steamed fish, boiled chicken, rice.'

'I'll ring my sister. She lives nearby and she's great in these emergencies. She's been coming in to check on Cha while Mrs Ames is on holiday . . . It was extremely good of you to bring Cha home and to look after her. You should have rung my sister to collect her from school instead.'

Mrs Shaw, her elbows on the table, drank tea. The moment of pause made him think that perhaps Mrs Shaw had gathered from Cha that she was not keen on her Aunt Alison.

'She's in my form and it was no trouble. It's one of the rare days when we are overstaffed.'

'It was extremely good of you,' he repeated. In the sitting-room the tall case clock chimed, and he flung up his arm to see his watch. 'Oh God, I am going to be late. It's the post mortem.' He could say so to the biology teacher, to whom animal dissection must have been customary.

'You have to attend them?'

'Policeman's lot.'

'This case . . . is it an accidental death?'

'No. I'd better take Zig's litter tray upstairs and put out another fresh one for Tombola, before I go. Thank you very much for making tea. I was much in need of it.'

72

He wanted to stay in her company, refreshed and stimulated, but he must go. Post mortem. Discussion. Phone Alison, soon. Get someone to arrange an interview with Archangel? – probably not as necessary now. Things seemed to be well wrapped up.

As he thought this, the familiar, fleeting touch of doubt halted him. He couldn't see why, with Lamia Hervey under arrest. All the same, as he put out litter trays, said goodbye to Charlotte and once more warmly thanked Mrs Shaw—

'Grizel,' she said. 'A traditional Scots name. Short for Griselda.'

'It's charming,' he said, and saw her amused disbelief. 'Grizel. Then I'm Robert.'

'Robert,' she said with Scots precision. 'Will your sister be coming round here soon? I must be away to school myself.'

They stood, as if something else were being said, looking at each other still.

'Oh – you mustn't wait. Alison has a key, and goodness knows when she'll arrive. Cha will do fine. She seems much better. And, poor chick, she's very used to being alone.'

'Her friend Prue's on the expedition, or she would have come home with her, I'm sure.'

'Oh yes. Yes, Grue will be round this evening.'

'It's lucky Cha didn't go to the museum. It's no fun turning wambly in the wild wastes of Kensington.'

'Her game leg did her a good turn for a change.'

'Yes.'

There was nothing to keep him. He went down

the stairs, and she came down to the door with him to see him off, as Petra used to do. What with that memory and Grizel Shaw's effect on him, he could almost have turned, in the most natural way, to kiss her at the door; but of course he did not.

'Goodbye, then. And thank you.'

'Goodbye. And don't worry.'

Ferdy Foster was annoyed with him. It showed only in his using a coarser grade of sandpaper in voice production. Bone watched, or focused on the top of Ferdy's head during the explorations he still could not watch and did not suppose he ever would. Ferdy's tape recorder hummed, Ferdy's commentary proceeded drily. At the points of interest he raised treacle-brown eyes to Bone but allowed no emphasis to alter his factual account. Only when it was over and he was washing, and had handed Bone a medicinal swallow of brandy in a small beaker, he said, 'Provided you with something to worry about, have I?'

'Yes, Ferdy. You've turned my case back into a conundrum just when I thought it was tidy.'

'The perils of premature presumption, Robert.' Ferdy picked up the towel and turned round. '*Ah, what a dusty answer gets the soul, when hot for certainties in this our life!* I like a few uncertainties myself.'

'So do I. Not in my cases, though.'

'Prefer uncertainties in your private life? Brave man.'

'I don't prefer them there, in fact; that's where they are.'

★   ★   ★

74

Cha was asleep and the flat felt unduly silent and empty. Bone had to fend Ziggy from the kitchen door as he went in. Tombola had eaten nothing more but had, with touching good manners, in using the litter tray covered his offering with the grey granules very carefully. He shifted awkwardly in the basket as Bone picked it up, in a balancing act that seemed likely to wrong-foot Bone and make him stumble.

Ziggy reared up to sniff the basket as Bone carried it past him, sniffed with ears up and eyes wide and wary; prolonged sniffing gave him Tombola's bouquet, while hostile sibilants from the basket showed Tombola's dislike of being on alien territory. Bone went downstairs carrying Alex Hervey's cat. A post mortem always gave him a sense of the pity of the inert and helpless dead.

Ziggy watched through the banisters, swinging his tail in wide, politely dismissive arcs, no doubt cat language for *piss off*.

Locker registered mild surprise at the tenanted basket as Bone stowed it on the floor in the back.

'You remember Emily Playfair in Saxhurst on the Nanny Gray case? She says she'll have pity on this one and put it up until it's found a home. It's Hervey's cat.'

'Another cat to her would be neither here nor there, I'd say,' Locker agreed, starting up. 'Wasn't the count fifteen when we were there?'

'That did include kittens. I could have handed this one to the RSPCA but they've enough to do. Ditto Chelsea police who'd have coped if they had to but made no secret of not being eager. But I'd thought of Mrs Playfair by then.'

Bone wound the window down to get rid of the disinfectant haze that still hung about him. A heavy waft of pig manure came flooding in and he laughed, winding it up too late.

'Any surprises in the p.m., sir?' Locker asked when it was safe to open one's mouth again. Bone wound down the window on a mown-grass smell as they turned off on the A262.

'M'm.'

'Funny old case, really. And an odd lot at Cryer's, bunch of nutters. What I felt by the time I'd got through just the ones that stayed overnight, was that any one of them could have done it. The pair I've just seen were no better. Live in another world, they do. And then, bingo, it all sorts itself into a domestic, you could say, wife shoots straying husband.'

'Not so simple when the husband's in a skirt and the wife believes she's shooting his girl-friend.'

'Could she really not know it was him?'

'People see what they expect to see. She'd got a real killer-bee in her bonnet—'

'I like that, sir.'

'Thanks.—Here was her husband enticed by the dazzling girl she was never allowed to see; and she was out to make them both sorry. I believe she even meant only to threaten, but she thought the woman was laughing at her.'

'Could she think she'd get away with it?'

'She'd arranged to be there under a false name. God knows what these people think. Sometimes they seem to have just about caught up with the fact that we can trace fingerprints.' Bone yawned. 'She said she threw her gun into some bushes on the way to London.'

'Threw the gun . . .?' Locker's forehead became ridges that ascended steeply to his hairline. 'What about Cryer's gun? It's been fired. Ballistics have got it.'

Bone pursed his mouth like one with a secret.

'Am I supposed to say "please"?'

'Ferdy tells us that Hervey was shot twice; once with a gun that from the bullets is probably Cryer's, and once with another of smaller calibre, presumably the wife's. She got around to shooting him when he was already dead.'

Locker's hands jerked on the wheel, taking them close to a burly, grey-bearded cyclist in shorts, with large furry legs, who bawled 'Pigs!' after them as they sped on towards Saxhurst.

Tombola, feeling the strain, uttered a muted echo behind them.

CHAPTER SIX

'So unless she first shot him with Cryer's gun, it extends our list of suspects comprehensively.'

'Square One,' Locker said, resigned. 'What about this monster thing? I couldn't follow what Cryer was saying this morning. A church object, isn't it? What is it doing in his room, then?'

'As I understand, it's a thing you keep the wafer of bread in, and show it to the congregation. Cryer says it could be put on a pole for processional carrying through the streets. Monstrance, demonstrate.' Bone's year of Latin at school brought the connection jumping to his mind as delightfully as the answer to a crossword clue. Locker eyed him, and he went hastily on, 'They can be very fancy indeed to look at, Cryer says. People used to load them with jewels to show they valued the wafer inside. Way of being devout.'

'So it's pricey? Really worth lifting?'

'Worth killing for, you mean? That is, if they're connected. God knows. Some people would say nothing is worth killing for, but it's human nature, that illimitably labyrinthine quality, to think your skin is more important than anyone else's. If the thief came for the monstrance, why did he unlock the drawer? Did he know beforehand a gun was there? How many people knew that?'

'I've tried to ascertain. It was an interview question and we may have results on it by now, sir; Pete Zed knew, his girlfriend Oriane Bligh says she did not. Sutton Somerton says he had no idea of it, nor did the other two. And what was Hervey doing in Cryer's room?'

'What was anyone doing in any of the bedrooms last night, Steve? Cryer had locked his room because he did not fancy any messy how's-your-father on that seventeenth-century bedspread.'

Locker shook his head, perhaps at the desecrated bedspread, and parked near the corner of Mouse Lane, the nearest he could get to Mrs Playfair's cottage in a Monday street full of the cars of shoppers here to stock up the freezer after the weekend. They were within sight of Mouse Cottage, standing there at the end of its brick garden path once bordered by the lavender bushes Nanny Gray had loved. The little cottage looked curiously bare without the protecting branches of the apple tree the new owners had cut down. Bone and Locker sat looking sourly at the trim display of ranked flowers planted the regulation six inches apart.

'You reckon a thief, sir?'

Bone sighed, so shallow and brief a sigh that he knew he was very tired. A dawn start to the day is apt to kick back around lunch time; the doze on the way to Chelsea had not appreciably helped. Ferdy's brandy had sharpened his vision painfully as though he were losing his energy to everything he saw. 'I don't dare to reckon anything, Steve. I have a feeling this isn't about to stop being a freak case.'

Locker shifted, but made no attempt to get out of the car.

'I haven't made out, sir, what this object,' he rather ponderously avoided naming it, clearly not being sure he had got it right or could get his tongue round it if he had, 'is doing in Cryer's bedroom if it does belong in a church. Is it a holy object? Would it be more common in an R.C. church? I never saw one in ours.'

'Cryer seems to have had it as a collector's item. He's fond of that sort of thing; you'll have noticed the carved wooden figure in the hall, and there are ikons.'

'And the crucifix over the stairs,' Locker added, mildly disapproving.

'You don't think he should keep stuff like that in a house.'

Tombola gave a low, pained cry from the back, serving in place of a comment from Locker. Bone smiled as Locker shrugged.

'You're not alone. Cryer showed me three letters from a bloke who thought just that.'

'This Brown Brother?'

'Can't help seeing him in a cowl and habit, like something out of a horror film, the Ghost of the Manor. His ideas are distinctly House of Blood too: Cryer, in his book, is to end up doing his fair share of hell in a hundred interesting positions, assisted by a herd of devils with heavy-duty pitchforks.'

'This is for having church things in the Manor?'

Locker frowned, and tapped his fingers on the steering wheel. 'Well, if he didn't steal them and isn't putting them to bad use, I don't see . . .'

A small boy, rattling a stick along the newly-white palings of Mouse Cottage, suddenly appeared to see watchers inside the car and, as if he knew they were police, ran headlong away across the road to a cacophony of car horns.

'—I don't see it's actually wrong. You'd have to be obsessive or very pious to mind; and death threats are another matter entirely.' He shook his head. 'It goes a lot too far.'

'Murderers do. Look, let's get a bite to eat before the conference. The case is wide open again. I'll take the cat and see if Mrs Playfair's in now. She said she should be by this time.'

Bone was leaning into the back to hoist Tombola out when he caught a wistful look in the face turned from the driver's seat, and said, 'Come on in, greedy-guts.'

They walked back along the road and, opposite the phone kiosk, saw the gate post heraldically occupied by a calico cat supervising the traffic.

The front door opened as they advanced up the path and Emily Playfair stood back waving them in. Her very dimples seemed to convey pleasure at seeing them.

'It's far too long since you were here. Yes, in the sitting-room. You've brought the cat.'

Bone felt tall in this house, as the beams were so near the top of his head and Emily herself was neatly small.

'Tombola.'

'Sit down, Mr Bone, Mr Locker. I've moved your chair over there, Mr Locker.' Steve, who had been having doubts about the small turned chair that had seemed to offer itself, moved to the sturdy upholstered one near the window. 'I tell you what I'll do, I'll put Tombola in the dressing room on his own for a while, to acclimatize. He'll have to be fed separately for a while in any case. They'll *eat* with strange cats if they're hungry, but they're so nervous that up it all comes. And then only a dog would eat it.'

Bone insisted on carrying the cat basket upstairs, to a very small room overlooking the back garden, with a cushioned window-seat and a cane planter's chair. This last was covered with a much-pulled blanket of patchwork knitting, and its leg-wrappings had come unsprung and looked like a dancer's leg-warmers. Mrs Playfair's deft ringed hands unlatched the basket and lifted the wire door off. She fished Tombola out. Surprisingly, he did not resist, but he cast Bone a surly glare.

'He's a beauty! A fine cat! Don't worry about him at all, Mr Bone. I can house him for as long as he needs.' She held his unresisting bulk against her, and her hands caressed. He bore it rather than responded, but when she lowered him into the basket, he at once came out and began to skirt the walls, sniffing. 'There,' she said. 'He will soon be at home. I'll bring all that he wants up here, directly minute.' The country phrase was apt in this old house. On the way downstairs she said, 'And you're tired and hungry.' She looked up at the bend of the stairs and her eyes twinkled. 'I've a pork pie and salad, and then there's a cake. I'm sure your Steve Locker could, as they say, use some of that. I made it because I was sure someone was coming today, but I didn't know then that it was you. And you can tell me about Tombola and why he's an orphan. I'm glad it was you who was coming.'

It was the second time in under twelve hours that someone had said *Nice that it's you*. Bone, warmed, followed her into the sitting-room, letting her dismiss his half-hearted protests and his talk of a pub lunch, especially as Locker was eloquently silent.

'Is Tombola connected with this unhappy death at the Manor?'

'He belonged to the person who was killed.'

'Ah, poor creature,' she said in a whisper. Whether she meant Hervey or Tombola, Bone could not tell. He and Locker sat in near-silence while she, again dismissing their formal offers of help, was busy in the kitchen. Her voice, talking to cats, kept background accompaniment. There was a very large black cat, with the bloom of brown that comes to black cats with age, heaped on the sofa. He had not moved, and did not move except for the steady heave of a rounded side.

Traffic went by. Arletty, a slim cat, came in and investigated Bone's feet and ankles, then Locker's. A gravid chinchilla walked through, her belly swaying, paid the silent men no attention, and went out into the hall.

Mrs Playfair returned, propelling a trolley and escorted by a brindle, the calico, and four tabby kittens. She set up the leaves of the gate-legged table and laid it, and then, with a ceremonious bow that mocked the real hospitality she was offering, she invited them to the table.

There was rosé to accompany the pie and salad, and hot home-made brown bread rolls. After a few minutes, Bone felt himself to be re-entering the human race. He could look about, appreciate the taste and smell of food and, seeing Emily Playfair was regarding him with her head on one side and an enquiring watchfulness, he could smile. In a swift gesture she tapped the back of his hand.

He wondered if she had diagnosed his state from obvious outward signs – was he too abstracted? vague? silent? – or from her own particular powers. She was exchanging a smile now with Locker and trying to refill his glass, while he said he was driving.

'There's the young Wheatleys,' she said, pointing out strolling teenagers on the far pavement, eating ice cornets. 'Their grandmother has been so much more able since they popped a new hip joint in. We went to Prestbury in the spring on a house-and-garden visit with the Crumblies' Club. The organizers keep trying to call it the Senior Citizens' Circle, but, poor pets, they're only middle-aged and haven't much of a clue.'

'Is that where Noel Prestbury lives?' He was the J.P. who had refused to talk to the team this morning; Bone meant to talk to him, very definitely, this afternoon.

'Yes, and it's a very strange house in its way.

Part of it is very ancient, and part of it nineteenth-century-medieval. No one would be able to treat an ancient house like that today. Mr Prestbury took us round himself, and it's plain how he loves the place. But while we were just going up to it from the coach, I did one of my seeings. There was a monk standing in front of the long wall we found out later was the Chapel. He was looking towards us with such a kind expression, so I waved, and I thought he nodded, but then I saw the light, the slight shimmer round him and I wasn't surprised that the next moment he was not there. At least, he may have been there, but I wasn't in touch any more. The trouble was, I'd mentioned him to Mrs Wheatley before I realized he wasn't actual, and she told Mr Prestbury. I don't like it to be talked about, but she was so excited that she forgot.'

She cut into the cake, a dark rich fruit cake glowing with cherries, and turned it towards Locker. For Bone she cut a less magnificent slice, with good judgement for his capacity.

'Still, it made him happy. He took us right into the Chapel, which he doesn't normally show. It is built on the remains of the monastery that was there before the house. Afterwards he wrote to me asking if I would go there and, I gather, sniff around for anything supernatural. He would fetch me, he said, in his car, and so on. But I never do such things. I told him that I have never, and do never, try to see; either it happens or it doesn't. Sometimes places trigger me off, and sometimes people. Robert for one; I latch onto things connected with you very easily, it appears.'

'You did that when we first met, about Nanny – Miss Gray.'

'Are you very intuitive yourself, Robert?'

'A policeman develops something of a nose about things, but that's all. Custom, and training, over the years.'

Locker said, 'That could be the cart before the horse, Super. I mean, a good copper gets on because of having a good nose.'

'But there's nothing psychic about it,' Bone protested.

'I didn't mean that,' said Locker hastily.

Emily cut the cake again. 'Of course you can manage more, Mr Locker. It's very nourishing. In your job you never know when next you'll get a proper meal.' She gave a neat little smile of satisfaction when Locker showed willing. 'Mr Prestbury was rather tiresome, though. It seems he told a journalist about me. A young woman turned up on the doorstep and said he'd told her all sorts of poppycock about my seeings and she wanted an interview. I sent her to rightabouts, I did indeed. To begin with, it was impertinent. And then, I didn't like her. There was something . . . false? I don't know.'

Alix Hamilton, thought Bone. Locker's eyes tried to catch his above the cake.

'Do you mind if I pop up and see Tombola? I think he wants something. Perhaps only a moment's company.'

'Of course, poor beast,' Bone said. He thought, however, that she might have latched onto Tombola's connection with the 'woman' who had called at her door.

She was back in a moment, almost before Locker had time to comment on Prestbury and 'Alix Hamilton'.

'Needed a cuddle,' she reported. 'Later on I'll introduce him to some of the others, the peacable ones first, but not till he's slept on my jersey.'

Bone wondered at this esoteric rite of *sleeping on the jersey*. His imagination had started a full ceremonial: the Placing of the Jersey; the Induction to the Jersey; Injerseynation.

'Then he'll smell friendly to them.'

'I see,' Bone said gravely. She had cut more cake and turned the plate towards them once more. Bone's knuckles clashed with Locker's, bringing to his notice that he was taking a slice. Its rich, nutty, moist, sharp sweetness enticed him to unusual greed. He said, with some thought of the religious aspect of the Hervey case, 'What sort of chapel is it at Prestbury?'

'It's surprising, really. There are choir stalls occupying the place where the brethren once were, about a dozen of them, and then a family pew, and you never saw anything more cosy. It has a little fireplace, and Mr Prestbury said that when he was a boy the curtain rail used still to be there, that held the baize curtain shutting the family off during the sermon. I thought, you could toast marshmallows if the sermon went on rather. But Mr Prestbury was quite earnest, no marshmallows, poor man. It seems that it can't be a proper chapel any more, and he does so mind about it.'

'Is he very devout?'

Mrs Playfair's alert gaze met his. 'Devout . . . I

may be unkind, but my impression was that what mattered was the insult to his house and family. The Host used to be kept there, which is what made it a proper chapel, so I understand, but when the old chaplain died, and he was ninety-one and had lived in the house since Shem, Ham and Japheth were boys, it had to stop. Mr Prestbury fairly roared out the history. Deaf, of course, and in that echoing place – a barrel ceiling; and he said quite violently that he had *stripped out* the chancel furnishings when the diocese refused the permission. When we got out again, Marian Wheatley said in my ear that the privilege of *that* private visit was one she could well have done without, her feet got so cold. Poor man, and *he* was so heated. What tragedies we make for ourselves.'

'Be a better world if we never made them for others,' Locker remarked.

'That would put you and me out of a job,' Bone said, rising.

Mrs Playfair, in the hall, thanked him for bringing Tombola, pre-empting his thanks to her. 'A lovely cat. Bewildered, but very willing.' She opened the front door, and said, 'Hallo, Tracey.'

A girl of about fifteen, in sawn-off and carefully frayed jeans and a teeshirt that stopped just below the bust-line, her hair pulled through a ring on top of her head so that the frizzy ends cascaded in all directions, said morosely, 'Gran says you needn't fetch her, because the doctor's been in an accident and he can't see her today.' She was the girl they had seen with the ice-cream across the road, so Bone supposed 'Gran' to be Mrs Wheatley.

'Thank you for coming to tell me.'

'That's all right,' Tracey said charmlessly, and took herself off down the path.

'What sort of accident?' Mrs Playfair called.

'Dunno,' said Tracey, going out at the gate.

'Poor Dr Walsh. I hope he's all right. Such a good doctor, with plenty of time for the crumblies. Tracey doesn't care for him, though. She had a nasty virus in the winter, and he came along because she was running such a temperature, and it seems she had a shrine in her room, candles burning before a picture, and I think incense, Marian told me – but she does ramble; and so do I, though you're so polite and don't say so. Dr Walsh took one look at this construction, all in front of a poster of James Dean – is that right? James Dean? – and he was perfectly furious and tore it all down. When Marian told me, I thought it was because candles and incense in a sickroom would choke up the air, and Tracey's room isn't very big and she keeps her curtains drawn all the time. But no! It was the idolatry. Dr Walsh gave her a sermon on the spot, it appears. He's a Protestant, though. Mr Prestbury's R.C. I can perfectly well remember how insane I was about Cary Grant.'

She made a prim mouth, but the irrepressible sparkle was there. 'Or was it Clark Gable? Goodbye, Robert. Bring Charlotte when you can. Goodbye, Mr Locker. Steve, then. Thank you.'

As they reached the car, and Locker fitted himself behind the wheel, he said, 'Funny thing about Mrs Playfair, she rambles on in a way that'd drive you up the wall if it was anyone else.'

The conference was held in the courtroom; blue shirts and notebooks, WDC Fredricks in a dazzling white blouse in a ray of sunlight, a PC with hay fever whose random bursts of three – always three – sneezes interrupted proceedings from time to time; the Office Manager, statement readers . . . and, Bone thought, *the great Panjandrum himself*, me, *with the little round button on top*; and we all are playing catch-as-catch-can . . . I must see if Charlotte still remembers that old nonsense-piece.

They went through what they'd got: Alex Hervey, dressed as a woman, found by Ken Cryer in his bed, in a room with a picked lock. Body shot two distinct times: one close shot penetrated left lung, tracheae, right lung, right arm; bullet, thirty-two, calibre of the gun kept in bedside drawer, gun now with Firearms. Second shot after death, from presumably bedfoot straight into chest, bullet twenty-two calibre, lodged in anterior surface of seventh thoracic vertebra; see statement of Lamia Hervey, widow. Body bruised on shoulders consistent with hand grip. Scratch on right index finger and palm, shortly before death.

Body clothed in suspender-belt, nylon stockings, jockstrap, slightly padded brassière, dress in gold metallic cloth, wig (long-haired, blonde), earrings of screw type. Here were photographs and this is the video recording again.

The photographs, the video, showed 'Alix Hamilton' sitting against the pillows, the bed-spread neatly over her legs. The dress's long sleeves in lily shape covered her wrists, a cowl neckline disguised the neck.

Lamia Hervey, wife of deceased, had confessed to second shooting. She had been as yet unable to state where, on the road to London, she had jettisoned the automatic pistol. She had said it fired once and had then been empty. She had supposed it was fully loaded.

Bedroom door had been opened with picklocks found in garden. Slight hilarity at this point elicited an explanation that they had fallen from a bush on to PC Wilkins' head as he searched beneath. Locked drawer also picked. Safety lock on bathroom cupboard had been tampered with but not opened. No other doors or drawers locked.

Rubber shoe prints in adjoining bathroom showed someone had stood against door for some time. WC had been used but not flushed, and thumb print under seat traced through HOLMES as that of Michael Gary Parsons, eighteen months for breaking and entering concurrently with eighteen months for possession of stolen goods, two snuffboxes from private collection, previous good character.

An article of value, namely a monstrance – picture, please – thank you; this was Ken Cryer's record of it – was missing.

Had everyone the copy of guest list?

Reports; questions; sneezes (always followed by 'Sorry, sir').

'What about Ken Cryer, sir?'

'He had opportunity and means. Could have picked lock as a blind or employed Parsons to pick it and to open bedside drawer likewise. No motive so far. He met the deceased on June 8th when as Alix

Hamilton he called to discuss writing an article about the house. No further contact, according to his statement, until the deceased was brought to the party by Jay Tansley-Ferrars yesterday evening.'

'Have we a gay killing, sir?'

'Information so far,' said Bone, 'is that Alex Hervey was heterosexual so far as the actual sex went. Cross-dressing is a borderline thing. Tansley-Ferrars says Hervey did it for a joke.'

'Might some gay have made a pass and, if he wouldn't, have killed him?'

'Possibly; but then they'd have tried it on only if they'd known he was a man, and apparently he was good enough for no one to spot it.'

'And Parsons, sir?'

'Very possibly. The lock-picking has the look of a pro job. As a scenario, he may have been disturbed during a search of the room, hidden in the bathroom, come out when he thought the coast was clear, have gone on searching, got to the drawer and seen the pistol, then realized he was being watched from the bed and shot Hervey to avoid being identified.'

The sneezer lifted a hand. 'I was in court when he came up for possession, sir. For what it's worth, he looked more the type who'd scarper than who'd shoot.'

'I don't like the scenario much either,' Bone said, raising a muted laugh.

'Can anyone tell me why Parsons hasn't been found yet?'

The laugh stopped dead.

'Now, you've got the print-out of statements so

far. Approximate times of guests leaving. You'll notice the general exodus was towards four. Here's Gwyn Griffiths, video director, looked into that bedroom at perhaps one in the morning wanting a vacant bed but saw someone was there; bedside light on, the woman in the gold dress, whose name he didn't then know, sitting up in the bed. He said "Sorry" and left. The woman didn't reply, which he thought rude. The girl with him, Susan Renoir, did not see round the door, but agrees the bedside light was on and says she smelt a "chemical smoky" smell. She thought there was "an earring or something bright" on the carpet at the foot of the bed, and pointed out on the room plan the spot where the twenty-two cartridge was found. Lamia Hervey left at 12.35, not taking leave of Cryer but saying to Mel Rees, who opened the gate for her, that she felt too tired to stay. He thought she'd had a row with whoever she'd come with, and left it at that. She'd come with Sutton Somerton, who had to stay overnight in consequence, but who denies any quarrel; and putting a bullet in someone would, I think we can take it, cause an appearance of agitation.'

'Suggesting,' Locker said, 'death at about 12.00, which is well within Dr Foster's hypothesis.'

'Did no one hear the shots? It's pretty hard to believe that no one heard them.'

'Ever been to a disco?' Locker asked.

'Well . . .'

'Think of hearing a shot from upstairs some distance away in the same building. There was champagne being opened frequently; you'll notice

93

the couple, Oriane Bligh and John Tanner, thought they could have heard shots, or a shot, but they were in a bedroom near the head of the stairs and thought it was champagne; so did Jem Cryer, who heard "Champagne going off like fire-crackers" but no shots at all.'

No one had mentioned the name of Mark Ser-afin among the guests, and perhaps not everyone present would connect it with the far wider-known stage name of Archangel. Now someone said, 'A whole group left at one o'clock and so far haven't been interviewed.'

'I've been trying to get in touch,' said Sergeant Shay, aggrieved. 'Trace of that lot – they're in London, but what parish no one knows. The record company keep saying they'll ring back. I've tried the *New Musical Express* for a home address, but Serafin hasn't one in London. They suggested the Dorchester, who say he's not there. I've tried every big hotel.'

'I don't think we'll get any joy from his record company,' Bone agreed. 'Anyone with a property like Archangel isn't going to want him connected with a police case. That's publicity they don't need. I'll look at that in a moment.'

'Inspector Blane is on a search of Hervey's house and is moving on to his flat, sir. The Chelsea people have been very co-operative.'

'I'd like to take Mrs Hervey on a drive after dark to see – belt up, you filthy-minded scum – to see if she can recollect where she threw the gun.'

Bone said, 'It might work.'

★　　★　　★

Bone rang the Manor. He got Edwina Marsh, her voice cheerful and with no trace of fatigue.

'Yes, I'm sure you can help me. As you can imagine, I need to have Serafin's statement, and others of his party; and he's gone to ground.'

'Wow. He would. He's got tonight's concert and then straight to the plane for the States. Leave it with me. I'll see what I can do. I've got the incident room number and I'll call back.'

While he was talking to her, his sister Alison rang. Cha was well, had eaten a boiled egg and was asleep again. Alison would go in again later and he need not worry.

He hoped Alison had not fussed Charlotte.

Alison was the only person ever to have called him Bobsie, and she had invented, some years ago, the name Charlie-Warlie for his daughter, who found it roughly as attractive as a plague of fleas. Still, her robust affection was a balance to his own diffidence. He could not help an unworthy joy that Cha preferred the diffidence.

'So, Steve: we have two men who, to put it reasonably, are earnest about religion. Prestbury, who's R.C. and deprived of his chapel and has criticized Cryer's possessing the monstrance, and I'd like to see any typewriter he has access to—'

'The Brown Brother's a bit warm about Cryer as a fornicator, too; unless that's all part of the reason why he shouldn't have the monstrance. The Pharisees were on a bit about Jesus and sinners, weren't they?'

'True. There's a dislikeable quality about right-eousness that's got it a bad name. Then we've Dr Walsh who tore down Tracey's shrine.'

'So far as we know, Dr Walsh didn't dislike "Alix Hamilton" and Prestbury very much did.'

'But could he have been surprised by the "woman"? Did they meet? Walsh was in the right place and at the right time, and he left in a hurry. They're both prone to violent actions; Prestbury stunned a hunt protester last year, and he was in a state with the "woman" that evening. Say he pursues her upstairs, shoots her, grabs the monstrance—'

Locker picked up the photograph. 'Nine inches in diameter, and weight—'

'M'm.' Bone rubbed his chin, the incipient stubble under his fingers reminding him how early that morning, and how fast and skimpily, he had shaved. 'He wasn't wearing a poacher's jacket, I presume. He must be seen; we'll be off there.'

'So far no one else shows with a motive. I mean, Cryer's a very long chance; there's Parsons who could've been surprised.'

'Who else was there who knew Alix Hamilton?'

Locker glanced at the list. 'Archangel. Tansley-Ferrars. Cryer. Mrs Hervey of course did and didn't. Oh, and she's made formal identification of Hervey. She's very distressed, but it's relieved her mind, to say the least, to hear she didn't kill him. She almost expected to be let go when I told her, but I pointed out she had shot, if not killed, him.'

'We've only her word for it she didn't know who he was. Did Blane talk to this Jane woman who stirred up the trouble in the first place?'

'Jane Whittle. Yes, she showed him her sight-line of the mews flat. She doesn't believe the woman was Hervey. Says she'd have known at once because men and women walk differently.'

'How useful.'

'Then Parsons could well have had a jacket with poacher's pockets. Nothing more likely.'

'Collect the facts, Stevo, nothing but the facts. And collect Parsons a.s.a.p. Don't blind me with potential. Let's see Prestbury.'

CHAPTER SEVEN

Noel Prestbury was waiting for them when they arrived, standing at the entrance to the deep brick porch. The front of the house was so pinnacled, turreted, so full of chevroned brick and loaded with Jacobean chimneys, bulging engaged pillars like dropsical legs embedded in the brick, as to suggest an architect drunk on Pugin Gothic. It was a wonder how Prestbury, himself a confessed devotee of antiquity, could be reconciled to living with anything so wholly *neo*-Gothic.

He let them come up the shallow steps before greeting them. At courts of the past, strict etiquette governed who came as far as the entrance hall to greet whom, and who was so exalted as to be escorted to the door of their carriage and watched out of sight. Evidently, Prestbury's refusal to speak to the team meant that Bone rated being met at the door, or even *outside the door*; but this might be merely the result of temperamental impatience. As they walked in, Bone had begun his professional appraisal: is this the murderer?

He had expected a face of character, with strongly marked features, and here it was; a noble head, the beaky, rather battered profile, grey-white, short-cut hair. A stone eagle above the door almost wickedly presented the same concentrated but aimless ferocity. Yet the eyes, disconcertingly dark and round under heavy lids, slid sidelong at Bone as they walked into the hall, curiously sly.

'Nasty business all this. Cryer must be cut up about it. Nasty end to his party. Rumours all over the village, my man tells me. Mrs Painton comes to "do" every morning and brings the shopping. We get gossip with the vegetables. Be in all the papers tomorrow. Change for them to have a story they don't have to make up. But I don't suppose we can expect the truth of it to appear in the Press.'

The hall, dark, high and large, was hung with the heads of dead animals. Two whose faces Bone could see looked decidedly annoyed, as well they might be. There were jade green and yellow encaustic tiles on the floor, the pillars supporting the stairs and first-floor gallery, and the walls; the effect was between a baronial lavatory and an ogre's larder. Their footsteps echoed.

The room they entered was vast, a product of that embarrassing and unconsummated love affair between the Victorians and their romantic vision of the Middle Ages – beloved for so many wrong reasons, or for qualities that did not exist. Bone, for whom architecture was a perennial interest, was fascinated. His attention, caught by the huge shallow arch of the chimney piece, dropped rapidly to a large rumbling wolfhound that had risen in a straggle of rangy limbs and was advancing on inspection duty.

'*Sit*, Garth. Don't make any sudden movements, Bone, he'll take your hand off at the knee.' Prestbury had a galvanic laugh that didn't affect his observant, malicious eyes. Who said, indeed, that people choose their dogs to project their image of themselves?

Garth swung his head away, disillusioned once more at being prevented from attack, and went to collapse in front of a vast fortification of a hearth deep under the chimney arch. It was set in what could only nominally be designated an inglenook, since the words suggest a restricted corner. This was a smallish room, with carved settles and a Turkey carpet like the reflection of flames.

He was not, however, ushered to the ingle but given a straight-backed chair at a refectory table. Prestbury took the head and, sitting in a dominant pose, turned towards Bone in a way that cut out Locker, and said, 'Well now. Tell me all the facts.'

Bone kept his temper. He was dealing with a J.P., and if the man thought the police were reporting to him rather than interviewing, that could be managed. Bone told again what he had told the Press: that Ken Cryer had found the body in a bed at the Manor after the party, and had informed the police, who were treating it as a murder enquiry. The deceased was fully clothed, wearing a gold dress, and was believed to be Alix Hamilton, a research assistant.

Prestbury shook his head.

'Bad business. I'd met her before last night.' He had a curious voice, upper-class, picking at his words. He did not shout as he had done at Emily Playfair; perhaps he had thought Mrs Wheatley to be deaf. In Bone's recollection she had looked not only deaf but daffy, a misleading impression.

'An unpleasant young woman,' Prestbury said, shaking his head. 'I quarrelled with her, y'know.' The eyes rose to Bone sharply, the eyebrows twitching. 'The fellow she works for has a name for himself, it appears, but when she came here, a couple of months ago, I had no idea that the object of the exercise was mockery. Naïve no doubt. Took her interest to be genuine. Showed her the place, of which I may tell you I am proud. And the piece he wrote was disgraceful. Very modern no doubt to make fun of sincerity and religious feeling.'

He paused. Another swift glance, that seemed to check the effect he was having on Bone, but may have been meaningless.

'Well. Last night when we met, told her what I thought. I was intemperate, Bone, in more senses than one, y'follow me? Not the thing at a social affair – though who, these days, knows or cares about that?'

'I understand you had had words with Cryer before that, over religious matters.'

'Told you that, did he? Well, his sort don't know what is decent. Get up and posture on a stage in front of screaming children. But after all, Cryer's a neighbour and one has to get along with people. I try to move with the times. No personal compromise, you understand. Have my own standards. Cryer's not a bad fellow but he has the moral sense of his tribe. Of course he can't understand how a Catholic would see these things. An object, a vessel which has held the body of Our Lord is not a suitable ornament. I told him so.

Cryer couldn't see it. Couldn't or wouldn't. I left the house. However, on consideration, I wrote to him. Apologized for the manner but not the matter. He accepted that, and on those terms he asked me to last night's affair. That's a fair account of it all, I think. But people no longer see the values that once were universally respected. As a J.P., I see it very clearly.' He added, with a sidelong look, 'As an instance, the way the police are regarded.'

Bone said, 'Indeed, sir. It's fortunate for us that you were at the party, since we need an informed opinion – people's attitudes, you know, and anything that you noticed. We should like to have an experienced judgement.'

He was not above flattery. He settled himself back in his chair, expanded a little. 'Well, I can tell you about one of the guests. Calls himself by a blasphemous name and looks no better than a pansy. Surrounded by sycophantic creatures, a crowd of punks.'

A convenient word for one generation to use of the styles they did not appreciate in the young. He could not envisage Archangel with a cockatoo-dyed crest and slashed clothes, razor-blade earrings and swastika tattoos; Prestbury very likely meant only that he thought Archangel's hair was not a natural colour.

'The country – this county in fact – is full of old houses decaying, while the money's in the hands of these screeching so-called singers. Cryer's rescued the Manor well enough, and it's damn well kept. He has a certain appreciation but utter blindness about religious matters. Divorced, you know.'

Bone looked attentive but said nothing. He knew Cryer's wife had left him some years ago, and he supposed that, according to the rules Prestbury still went by, Cryer ought not to have allowed her to divorce him.

'What else was there of note, sir? Was there any other incident involving the young woman?'

'If there was, I didn't see it. Only myself!' The galvanic laugh again, like a machine abruptly thrown into motion, abruptly stopped. 'Well, you can hardly consider me. I admit I thoroughly detested the woman, but *de mortuis*—' he flashed that glance at Bone, doubted his Latin, and finished pompously, 'We must speak nothing of the dead but good.'

'I'm not sure how easy that would be, sir. I think you should know a fact we're not at this moment making public, but which it is proper to tell you in confidence.'

'In confidence. I understand.' Prestbury did not say *you can rely on me*, and this confirmed Bone in his belief that he perfectly did understand official secrecy.

'Alix Hamilton was not a young woman at all, sir. She was the *alter ego*—' how's that for Latin? – 'of the writer Alexander Hervey himself. She was a man.'

Prestbury sat frozen. The round eyes kept steadily on Bone, the mouth came ajar, lizard-like. After a long moment he snapped his mouth shut and then barked, 'Damnable!'

A flush had come into his cheeks, an elderly man's mottled flush. Bone thought *he flirted with her; goosed her in the gallery*. Holding his face of quiet attention, he watched Prestbury's neck go red.

'Damned pervert. Disgusting! I agree with you! How can one think well of a man who – Vile! *Vile!*'

After a time for Prestbury's choler to fade a little, Bone enquired, 'When you say, sir, that you saw no one else of note, you are of course not implying that there was no one else there whom you know.'

'Know! Well, people one meets here and there. Lady Herne, something of a merry widow, hey? And Jay Pansy-Ferrars.' Prestbury barked briefly. 'Most of the rest I think were Cryer's own cronies. Some decent enough chaps and a few pretty girls. But pretty girls mess themselves about so now, with their hair all over the place . . . There was an architect fellow I've met before. Can't remember his name. And some others who were here when Cryer used the old kitchen garden for a television film he was making, but I can't recollect their names. Don't think I ever knew what they were.'

'Did you recognize Mick Parsons, sir?'

'Mick Parsons? Mick Parsons? Should I?' The head reared.

'He was up before you once. He works for Griffiths, the video director.'

'Oh. Rings no bell. But y'know, at that party I didn't see everyone to talk to, and they had the lights so low it was like a damned night-club. If Parsons was there perhaps he was avoiding me. Might think I'd warn Cryer to lock up the silver, hey?'

'I should imagine Cryer's a careful man, sir.'

When they left, Bone asked Locker for any comments. Locker sucked his teeth. 'I dare say it's coincidence, but he said "posturing" about pop singers, like the Brown Brother.'

'And you won't have missed that Emily Playfair saw a monk here and told Prestbury, or Mrs Wheatley did, that she'd seen him. How do you think of a monk as being dressed?'

'Could have given Prestbury ideas, all right. What about it, sir?'

'Would you say the language of those letters was intemperate?'

Bone yawned. Visions of pillows swam in his tired mind. The sleeping wolfhound had moved him to envy. He tried to recall another thing that had struck him during the interview.

'Parsons, now. What made Prestbury think that Parsons had been up before him for *theft*, if he could not remember him? He connects him with it. Had the name in the back of his mind at least.'

Reaching the incident room, Bone consulted his watch without in the least registering the time. He received the reports passed from the office manager, and a message. Edwina Marsh had contacted Serafin's secretary; the star would talk to Bone after the Wembley concert.

She had got in touch, with some difficulty, as Serafin always went to ground before a concert, somewhere private where he could not be reached. Bone experienced another stab of envy, and took a mug of coffee from Fredricks. She also put before him a large pale bun.

He smiled gratitude at her and steamed his face over the mug. Unsealing the vast bun, he glanced at its contents and found it freighted with mustard, also, lightly, with ham that trailed a sickly piece of rind like an elastic band. He was too tired to want food, but must eat to think. Extracting the elastic band, he put the bun together again, getting flour on his hands, his jacket, the telephone, and the reports; and ate.

When he could ring Charlotte he found she was up.

'How are you? You shouldn't be out of bed again.'

'Oh, I'm better. I feel well now. That was terrific stuff Mrs Shaw got me. No more pangs.'

'Are you sure?'

'Yes. Don't bother Aunt Alison any more. Prue will come soon and stay the night, can she?'

'Of course, if that's all right with Mrs Grant.'

'You *know* it always is. No sweat then. You will be back?'

'Can't say exactly when, pet. I'm off to Wembley.'

'Oh Pa! Not to the concert?'

'Don't scream at me. Not to the concert. I'm seeing the great man after it.'

'Get his autograph. Please, please do. Oh police have all the luck. You don't even *want* to see him.'

When Bone had replaced the receiver he palmed his eyes. Fredricks said, 'Your daughter wants to come too?'

'She tells me police have all the luck,' he said wryly. 'Ring Wembley, will you? Ask them to tell their men at the stadium we're coming, et cetera. Miss Marsh says Serafin's people are expecting us?'

'Yes. They were a bit emphatic about the time.'

'Have Powers standing by in plenty of time to get us there. He'll have to check with Roads.'

'Yes, sir.'

'I'm teaching my grandmother to suck eggs. Sorry, Pat.'

He went on reading. Insector Blane had talked to Mrs Hervey in the presence of her solicitor. Blane's report made clear that the man was a pain in the neck, objecting to the very thought that his client could be capable of murder. Blane's team was still at work going through Hervey's flat.

The car carried Bone and Steve towards London, orbiting on the M25. Bone had thought he would sleep, the monotony of the road having worked on him that morning, but he could not. He tried to collate the accounts, to weigh motive . . . he observed that a piece of somebody's bad driving, allowed for and accepted calmly by Powers, roused him to hot irritation. It was fatigue. He knew the symptoms.

'Steve. Penny for?'

'Thinking about rock stars.'

'Thinking what?'

Steve made a face. 'Well, what a set. I mean, getting money of the sort they get for what they do. Research scientists can't get the funds, hospitals can't, and these blokes get it for just singing. It's a crazy set of values, see it how you like.'

'I bet they paid gladiators more than anyone

else in Rome, too. It figures. People will pay for pleasure.'

'But it's out of proportion. And this one, this Archangel. The way he looks is too good to be true. Got up the way he is and putting on his act.'

'Posturing, you mean?'

Locker grinned, 'Right. It's a sort of con trick played on the kids. They get to feel they have to have all the records all the other kids seem to be crazy about. I bet half of them or more don't like them that much. Archangel with his looks had it made, I'd say.'

'I wonder if looks in a man are even tougher than in a woman. Most men'd feel as you do, that going into show-biz was an unfair bid for attention, that the face is the only asset. A man using his face as his fortune.'

'I think it's pitiful.'

'You don't like pop music?'

'Ah well, no, that's going too far.' Steve's hand came up in protest. 'There's a lot of good tunes, and some of the songs have a lot of sense or maybe a lot of feeling. But I admit, this Archangel puts my back up.'

The streets of Wembley were all but empty, and had a certain melancholy under the streetlights, an air of being nowhere, abstracted from the real action. Bone could feel as much as hear the sound above the car's engine, a vast heartbeat, eerie although he knew what it was. They sped up the vein towards that furiously active heart, the volume growing. At least one couldn't doze off here, any more than catch a quick kip in Hell.

They paused, the driver spoke from his window and was directed. They crawled into a tunnel, threaded round in an inferno of noise that nobody could by any stretch of optimistic grace call music, a sound bellowing round them off the concrete surfaces, doubling itself so that it contradicted the steady pound of drums, magnified past the ears' ability to work it out, concussing, stupefying. Bone resolved never would he let Cha attend a pop concert. He thought, why had music to be raped like this, carried clean across the threshold of pain?

The car had stopped. People with badges were there, beckoning, pointing urgently. Bone hurried, sweat starting out in the airless heat, ears bursting at the pressure of huge sound, not only music but a yelling whistling roar from the thousands in there; his heart out of sync with the vast heart of the drums. Steve, his eyes narrowed in pain, looked dazed as Bone probably did. They were signed towards a long silver car, handled into it with dumbshow of polite speed. A man in earphones with a walkie-talkie semaphored, the rear door was held open. The car's engine made itself felt, a counterpoint of vibration. Torches flashed, the roar of the crowd had, incredibly, risen and heralded a fantastic rush for the car. The driver's arm moved as he put it in gear; Bone flinched as two bodies flung themselves in beside him, the door slammed hard and the car had started with a surge like a launched missile.

The bodies restored themselves, as the car shot from the tunnel, into a white-haired man, out of breath and visibly exuding steam as if from a bath, a towel round his neck like a boxer, in a black lace teeshirt, a jacket white as his hair, and an almost tangible aura of energy. The other was a very tall brown girl in skin-fitting brown leather, her face under the sliding lights severely elegant. They passed barriers held apart for them, and all fell onto each other as the car swirled into a tight corner and bombed down a cleared stretch of street. Bone, pushing himself upright amid apologies, still breathless, from Archangel, heard the howl of the stadium behind them. He glanced back, almost expecting to see a pursuing horde, but saw only headlights; another of Serafin's cars and then Powers.

'I warn you I'm not coherent yet,' said the light voice encouragingly. 'But I will surely do my best. Still high,' he explained casually. His presence was almost a physical assault, as if he had been stretching his personality towards the crowd and had not yet retracted it. Locker seemed to have shrunk, perhaps to avoid this emanation. The smell was in fact a circus one, of greasepaint and animal glamour and danger, a touch of the great cats about it. Archangel towelling himself matter-of-factly seemed making an effort to crank down the sexuality as his breathing quietened. Beyond him the dark girl watched the street. This must be Mary Highmountain, the bodyguard.

Bone regarded Serafin with frank curiosity, waiting to start. The face's proportions were the determining factor of its appeal. Was there a geometry of the perfect, as in architecture the exact distance between window and roof and door that might land you with Georgian, or between eye and nose and mouth that might land you with Garbo or with this man? Or Alex Hervey for that matter. Ken Cryer had been struck by that disturbing likeness.

Serafin, too vigorous with the towel, caught the now forward-leaning Locker with the edge of it, apologized with blinding charm and turned to Bone. He visibly gathered himself to serious consideration of Bone's purpose.

'Poor Alexander. I was glad I had this performance tonight, it prevented too much thought about it. You'll tell me how I can help.' His eyes were dark and intense under the white (Bone supposed bleached) floss silk hair. He had not quite managed to reduce the stun area and still glittered, the charge set too high.

'Did you expect him to be at Cryer's?'

Serafin was, after all, a suspect. He had certainly the opportunity, or the agents, to kill Hervey, and as to motive, far the most murders were in the family. He briefly imagined anyone trying to deal with the tall brown girl, no doubt an expert in the martial arts, who sat so easily, confident of herself, as if capable of taking on any three men who were foolhardy enough to try it.

'I didn't. I didn't look to see either of him.' He stared at his hands in the towel, then ahead at the road past the driver. 'It's being aware two things are there at once, this someone being dead.' The hands, small and neat but square, came up before him one in front of the other, changed places. 'He's dead, which is one fact, and I don't take it in. All my life he's been living; so that I believe he's dead,

111

but I don't know it. You must be too used to this, m'm? and can allow for it. Now Cryer's, you asked about that. I saw him right when we arrived. He meant to be seen. That wig and dress. I thought, Ah, we are a woman, are we? Okay. There can't be many impersonators good as he was. The extra thing was that to him it was real, not theatre. In theatre the man wants you to know he's a man. He's taking off the feminine, a satire at best, a chauvinist joke at worst. In drag acts it's the glamour, the unreal that some gays see as the feminine. Alex played it on his own. He could become feminine, female.

'He was moving about a lot. Here there and everywhere. One old man up whose nose Alex had really got, calling him seven kinds of bitch. I said to Mary, "If he touches Alex, go and hold him", so she moved over. If he'd clouted Alex the wig might have shifted. Ah, but I've not introduced Running Gag: Mary Highmountain.'

Mary Highmountain bent her head in their direction.

'When eventually we talked, Alex said he was Old Man Kangaroo, well and truly sought after. He said his wife was there, as I'd seen. She is not a fan of mine; we'd had a brief encounter when I came in, but she kept it very cool. We're not on terms. She sees,' he pointed to his chest, 'a cheap exploiter. *I* see an expensive sloven. Alex was ready to spit because she was there. If she got close she'd know him and blow it. He said an old flame of his was there as well. He was pretty amused about it all. Later, we danced.'

112

Serafin's face had been familiar from the posters on Cha's wall, from record sleeves and shop displays, disbelieved automatically as product of the airbrush; you look at flower catalogues and discount the pictures, knowing the real flower will be brown at the edges, rain-beaten, victim of leaf curl and the caterpillar. Here, the real face had more than the posters, had life and movement. Bone, who had never met a beautiful man until now, was interested in the phenomenon.

'Was he there all the time you were there?'

'He wasn't in sight when we left. I looked to say goodbye.'

'What time would that be?'

Serafin turned his head to Mary.

'Twelve thirty,' said an American voice as deep as his.

'What made him dress and act as a woman?'

Serafin paused. They were out of streetlights now and he was almost down to life-size. 'I've always thought, his mother. She was one of these stunning women. My mother is a looker but her sister was out of this world. We both look like her. Alex saw the effect, m'm? the effect that a woman like that has on men, and Alex didn't have so much effect on his own. It's a matter of projecting. He had no scope or perhaps ability for it as a man.'

'You knew him well.'

'We saw a lot, each of the other, as kids, our mothers being sisters. Aunt Kika married this baboon face who was a top-class mountaineer and incidentally rolling in money, and they had Alex. He was for ever exhorting Alex to be manly, not

113

with marked success. Started with the wrong material.'

'How unmanly was Hervey?'

'As a masculine animal, normal. You don't ask if he was gay.'

'Was he gay?' Bone asked promptly.

'No. He was a lot more intelligent than his dad but he resented like hell being dragged to beginners' slopes in the Lake District every holiday and taken to football matches when he wanted to be reading. He used to skive off on his own, exploring. He knew about architecture from forever ago, I can't remember when it began. And history. After he married he settled in and wrote this heavy tome, magnificent research and hard slog, *Cross on the Door*, on the Plague. He was really living with it, and Lamia with her modelling was the money they lived *on*. They were happy and looked it . . . my dad subbed them a bit. Poor man, I was into rebellion at that time so I wouldn't touch his money.'

Mary Highmountain coughed absently.

'That's not the sort of personal history I give out with,' Archangel said, 'but Ken Cryer says you are a human being. I used to envy Alex having this real work, something worthwhile,' he went on, while Bone wondered what Cryer's remark signified. 'We all thought it would be a masterpiece, a milestone. He could write – he made it, all this history, quite absorbing. Well then, some established historian, a big name, produced an exhaustive, definitive book on the Plague that very same year.'

Archangel's whole body expressed collapse.

'The reviewers took them both and Alex's was treated as if he'd tried to get on the bandwagon. They said he trivialized, called his book the strip-cartoon version . . . a few recognized a gift, said the book was sound, but the general effect, Jesus wept; you know critics. Half of them are out to show themselves off, not to give a straight opinion; panning is clever. Alex was wiped out. He's written nothing worth while since. Smart stuff that makes him a living, the glossies, trivia. He's sold out. Well, God, you have to stand being knocked down. I felt terrible for him for a while, but you can't spend the rest of Time saying yes, how unfair, the world's a bitch. I've been back to the starting line often enough. And he thought my career was a cheap option, so we had a—' up came the hands again, palm to palm, and drew apart. 'But we got on, since basically we're very alike. He knew I'd go along with his cross-dressing, for instance, and I thought Lamia had turned into a ball-breaker long before he did.'

The car hummed in silence. Trees and hedges showed in the headlights. Archangel leant forward and opened a small glittering cupboard whose door made a shelf.

'I'm cool enough for a drink. Should have asked you before.' He perched on the edge of the seat and held up bottle and can. Bone accepted a beer. What was beginning to dawn on him was hunger, and he wondered how he had managed to miss a meal.

'Hervey made a good living from these books and articles?'

'Good enough. Lamia got past modelling – they boot you out in your twenties – and I always thought she should try to get a job, something she could do. Lately I had the feeling money was not keeping up with the lifestyle: house, flat, hired help.'

'Mrs Hervey said they had no help.'

Serafin laughed. 'Place must have been a pigsty, then. How is she? I phoned the house when I heard, but no answer.'

'She's under sedation.' Bone finished the beer, thought, and said, 'She shot at him under the impression he was her husband's girl-friend.'

Archangel's face turned towards him, lit by the cupboard's glow. 'Christ,' he said. 'Oh God, how ironic.' After a silence he went on, 'He'd have liked the irony,' and emptied his glass. 'He'd want to laugh. So it caught up with him at last. Did she find out what she'd done?'

'She didn't kill him, Mr Serafin.'

Archangel turned completely to face Bone, sitting sideways, intent. 'Then? Who?'

'Did he have enemies?'

'Enemies? Like that old josser at the party, there were a thousand people he'd got across. He could needle. Enjoyed it. He'd have made enemies that way. Part of his liking to – oh, manipulate. A power thing. That's what it was all about. I don't know. Not anyone who'd kill, m'm? It's not enemies that kill. I've had death threats; Ken's had them; they're not so likely to do it. The dangerous one is the one that comes out of nowhere with no warning and his mind blown.'

Bone took a deep breath. This was a mistake, for it made him feel more tired. The beer had not helped. Archangel's presence, bizarre as a meteor, confused his mind. The car sped towards the airport, where Archangel's plane would be warming up to carry him into the skies. There was a fuller picture of Hervey now, but what should he be asking, now with the time slipping away?

'Do you know who did shoot him, if she didn't?' Archangel asked.

'No. Can you pinpoint when you last saw Hervey?'

Archangel considered. 'Not easy to know it was the last time I ever shall. It was so casual.' He bit his lips, staring beyond Bone out of the window. Bone unwillingly was about to prompt him when he said, 'It can't have been long before we left.' Flinching, the eyes turned to Bone. 'Some time round midnight.'

'And you've no idea who "the old flame" was?'

'None. No clue. Not even if man or woman. It was just the sort of situation he enjoyed.'

Mary Highmountain said, 'But he looked across the room when he said it, at someone tall.'

'Well, Mr Bone, that's the sort of thing Laughing Gas is there for, to see everything.' Serafin put a hand on her thigh.

'Someone tall. You're sure?'

'Quite sure.' She was not offended. She could take trivial nicknames and aspersions on her accuracy of observation.

'Leaning Tower is there to watch. Looking for

anything out of line. Who was there last night at cloud level?'

She was there to watch. Thousands of news cameras caught the important people waving, smiling, while behind them always were the hard faces that did not smile, that checked the crowd for that wrong gesture, the move that threatened, the face that didn't fit. She was answering. 'One or two people were around my height. Ken's security man. Mick Parsons. That architect I spoke with.'

'That'll be Sutton Somerton, sir.' Locker, perhaps overwhelmed by Archangel and the woman, was subdued.

Serafin crowed a laugh. 'Sounds like some place off the M1. Think I met him too. A bloke who let me know he could redesign any of my houses at any time. Yeh, come to think of it, he was about level with Standing Jump here.' He put his hand on her thigh once more and turned towards her. Bone was aware, edgily, of his throwing the switch for her benefit, and wished he could reset it to normal social level. Clearly, sexual vibration existed independent of gender, and if Alex Hervey had possessed this particular force he must have made a formidable woman. To Bone it brought back the presence of Grizel Shaw sitting opposite him in the kitchen that morning, her vivid gaze, his sense of being alive when she was there. What did Locker, with his ideas of the manly, think of this super-charged atmosphere? Check Sutton Somerton with him; he'd interviewed the man that morning.

Serafin was speaking again, with affection in his voice. 'Mary is Cherokee, you know. Her tribe in the States elected a woman chief a couple of years back and do you know what her name was? Wilma Mankiller. I'm safe in this one's hands, though I speak with forked tongue.'

She said, 'I hear your words, white man.'

How much time was there left, with this car flowing smoothly through the night, the road unreeling beneath?

'Mr Serafin, can you tell me exactly what terms you were on with your cousin.'

Archangel's eyes were questioning, then understood. 'You mean, did I do it, or hire it done. Get Rising Gorge to sneak out and waste poor Alexander on the quiet? Sorry. It would get your name on the news all over the world, I see that. But no. So . . . We pulled each other's hair in girlish tantrums when we were kids, I even knocked him down in a quarrel – over, I think, a toy bear – but since then, only the friendly conspiracy against the world. And lately we've not met so often. I'll miss him. It's going to be a hole in life, I think. I'm going to have to look at it, come to terms.'

Mary Highmountain said, 'Write a song about it,' in her calm, indifferent tone.

This cruelty, a suggestion that his grief would be superficial, was met with only a serious glance and a nod.

'Probably. After a while. One of those I never sing.'

Bone's instinct, which had signalled more depths in Prestbury's account, told him now that

119

he had very likely heard the truth now. Whatever it was, his time was gone. The car was running among lights, was stopping. They had arrived. Mary Highmountain was out, uncoiling panther and snake, standing back and looking round. The guard held the door for Archangel. Bone and Locker ducked after. Bone, stiff and feeling clumsy beside the competition offered by Serafin and the woman, and by the rest of the entourage approaching, designer jeans, silk shirts, and salon-cut hair, wondered what he had not managed to ask.

Archangel was standing, waiting for him, the beautiful face pale in the airport lights, his hair pulled by the night breeze like dandelion floss. He was a man who'd have trouble not looking dramatic at any time and now, against the looming shape of his plane and the night sky he seemed to give the simple act of departure another dimension. A poem, a poem of Housman's that had haunted Bone in his romantic 'teens, came after all these years to his mind:

> *From far, from eve and morning*
> *And yon twelve-winded sky,*
> *The stuff of life to knit me*
> *Blew hither. Here am I—*

'Can I do anything else? Anything before I go?'

> *How can I help you, say,*
> *Ere to the wind's twelve quarters*
> *I take my endless way.*

Bone, confused and exhausted, stood unable to

120

think. Archangel stood patiently, his people bustling aboard the plane, his minders towering.

'My daughter,' Bone said. 'Can I – could I have an autograph for my daughter?'

'Mr Bone, I'd be delighted.'

He held out a neat hand, like someone who always had what he wanted instantly, and Locker, with an air of surprise, flipped his notebook and held it out with a pen. Taking it as it materialized, Serafin wrote on it, gesturing to Locker to support it; which Locker did, glancing at Bone as if to ask what he was doing playing desk to a pop star in the middle of an airport.

'Her name?'

'Charlotte.'

'Here. Give her my love. Tell her to go on buying the albums or I don't eat.'

Bone's stomach gave a muted roll of sympathy as he shook hands. Somewhere behind a barrier quite far away, people were wailing the star's name. Bone was attracting their envy and blocking their view.

'Goodbye. Hope you get your man. Or woman. My secretary will send you an itinerary, so you'll know where to contact me if you want to ask anything more.'

He was being drawn away, surrounded, moved to his plane by the minders. Bone, too, withdrew, going aside to where his car waited. Archangel waved from the steps to a renewed, frantic screaming from the fans. Locker was having rather cross words with an official questioning their presence. Bone watched the plane stand waiting and then move towards the runway. An experience, he thought. I wonder what the hell else I didn't ask. Trace, interview, eliminate. He had done the first two and virtually the third.

Locker tore out the page of his notebook carefully and handed it to Bone.

CHAPTER EIGHT

Home felt as if he hadn't seen it for months. He crept up the stairs. The cat Ziggy thrust a marbled head between the banisters to welcome him, and he gave a brief caress. On his way to Charlotte's room, he passed the open spare-room door, saw the light on and Prue Grant's tousled head on the pillow beside a book. He drew the door to, not wanting to wake her with his movements about the flat. Ziggy had gone in, and came out just as the door was shutting.

Charlotte's room was in darkness. He heard her light breathing and stepped in to put the autograph on the bedtable.

Ziggy went with him into his own room, but did not stay. Bone shut him out, not anxious to be woken early by Ziggy on the duvet. Images of the day whirled in his head as he undressed, went to the bathroom, got into bed. The airport food lay heavy on his stomach, but all the same he sank ineluctably deep, pleasurably, almost voluptuously, into sleep.

He woke because Ziggy had jumped on the bed, but it was daylight, it was nearly eight and Charlotte was there with a mug of tea. He sat up, to avoid Ziggy's investigation of his hair.

'Thanks. I need that very badly.'

'You got the autograph. I saw it first thing. *What* is he like?'

'You rustle up an emperor-sized breakfast, and I'll tell you if I can.'

'If? If? You damwell had better,' Charlotte said, and kissed him. Going out, she asked, 'Mixed grill?'

They were waiting; putting a dinner-plate before him and promptly sitting down with expectant faces, their school uniform frocks making them look younger than their own clothes would do. Prue was all eyes, teeth, intelligence, Cha more fragile, prettier, intent. He ate bacon, fried egg, beans and toast.

'Meals got erratic yesterday. I'm even ravenous after a snack at the airport. Sorry. Well, he's got a lot of what you could call animal magnetism. He's a neat, clever fellow.'

'How close did you get to him?'

'Close? I was next to him in his car all the way to the airport.'

They moaned. At this point he took in the significance of the Haddon House uniform and said to Charlotte, 'You're not going to school after yesterday.'

'Of course. I'm fine, it's only a half day and we do next to nothing. Go *on*.'

'I don't know what to say about him.'

'Oh Daddy you cheat. I cooked you a breakfast. You *said*.'

'I'll try, but . . . you know what he looks like, after all.' As he ate, he described the getaway, the noise, the eruption of Serafin into the car, and the fast exit.

'What was he wearing?' They leant their arms on the table.

Bone told them.

'Did you like him?' Prue asked.

'Yes. Yes, I did. It was – a friend of his who's dead.'

'Oh poor *thing*. Does he mind?'

'Yes.'

'But all the same he gave his autograph.' It was by Cha's plate in a plastic envelope. She spoke as if Serafin had fought back tears to write it.

'His friend?' Prue said. 'Woman or man? Was it a lover?'

Experiencing shock, and seeing none in Charlotte's face, he said, 'No. Someone he's known for years.' The girls were not surprised, much less disturbed, at the idea their idol might have a man as a lover. Where did innocence go?

'Was his bodyguard there? The Cherokee Indian?'

'Yes. Very impressive, I may tell you. She rode with us.'

'Was his girl-friend there?'

'I don't know. There were girls in the other car and they got on the plane.'

'What did you say when you asked him for his autograph?'

'I can't remember. I have a daughter who'd like your autograph, or some such.'

'What did he say?'

'He said, and I can tell I must get this right, he said "I'll be delighted!"'

'Delighted,' Cha whispered.

'Soppy,' Prue said to her. 'You are *soppy*.'

'And he sent you his love.'

'He did? He did really?'

'"Give her my love" he said.'

Prue's elbows thumped the table. She gripped her head between her fists. 'This settles it,' she said. 'I'm going into the police.'

On his way from collecting his jacket upstairs, he stopped at Cha's door. He looked at the walls, the posters of those he could recognize: Cryer, Bowie, Bono, Jagger, Archangel. The face was strange: static, frozen in the photographer's vision, dramatically lit, unreal.

He dropped the girls at school, telling Charlotte to look after herself, but she seemed cheerful and quite recovered. As he went on alone in the car, the case was instantly with him as if it had been waiting. This morning, however, fed and rested, he was optimistic. He thought over what he had got as he drove through the countryside. As a man of Kent he had a proprietorial sense of belonging, even though he came from the northern shore. He liked to be this side of the Medway, to thread along roads among the small towns, as now while the mist was still lifting and the horizons lay in successive washes of blue.

Most traffic was going the other way. No one, for a wonder, was ahead of him on Goudhurst hill and he could swing up it in top, slowing only as he came into the town itself. A coach was loading outside an inn with a party ready to tour. A shopkeeper put out her display. He made the tight turn at the church, saw the notice 'Tower Open' and recalled, sharp as a knife, climbing the tower with Petra and the infant Charlotte. Cha had wanted to climb on her own, indomitable child, but had given in to 'Mommy carry'. Fairly soon Petra had said 'Daddy carry', and they had come out at the top breathless, laughing, to see the miles of Kent around them in the sunshine, fields, hedges and woods, the nestling roofs. Petra had leant over the parapet to look at the tower foot, and stood back with a hand at her throat, pale. 'I've just discovered vertigo.' Bone had decided against looking down. They had stood in the bright air watching cloud shadows cross the world.

Memory had carried him on as far as the turn for Saxhurst. By association with the past, the crash, Petra's death, he had the irrelevant, bitter thought, *At least money's not tight any more*. The steady cost of Cha's therapy was over. She had only speech classes once a week, checks with the orthopaedist every month. Her spine was straight, her left leg as normal as it was likely to be. She spoke, to Bone's hearing, with perfect clarity, although Alison said she still slurred. Petra, phantom limb of their family, still pained him. He could not envisage a time when it would not, but had to acknowledge with guilt that it pained him less often.

Here was Saxhurst. Meaning to think seriously, he had not remembered the case for miles.

Now it absorbed him, drew him back as the smell of disinfectant, VDUs and scrubbed humanity surrounded him. Here was Sergeant Shay with the update, and with the computer chart of where everybody was around midnight. The only person nobody had failed to notice was Archangel, who had been there all the time. Everyone else seemed to have gone to and fro, vanished and reappeared, in any of the three rooms the party was in, up either of the two staircases to spend unspecified times upstairs; into the garden, to the bathrooms.

Fredricks reported that Sutton Somerton, who had stayed the night at Cryer's after the party, had not been home since. His wife had reported him missing, hysterically repeating that she was an invalid and helpless. She had read in the papers about the murder, 'and she seems terrified that her husband has been murdered too. She seems to think it's catching, as if anyone who'd been there was liable to drop dead of it.'

Fredricks hesitated.

'She sounded as if she might have been drinking.'

'If she's an invalid, it may be she has some illness that affects her speech.'

'Oh yes, sir. That may be it.' Fredricks sounded relieved, as if the imputation were regrettably uncharitable. 'I got in touch with the social services, anyway.'

Bone got together his small team for a progress and ideas talk. Locker had sent DC Brevis to Tenterden to collect a photograph of Somerton from the frantic lady, and had put out an alert. The description *six foot three, short dark hair, slight build, pale, rather protuberant hazel eyes, dark grey summer suit, blue tie*, he had supplied from his own interview with Somerton the morning before.

'Are we any forrader on things?' Bone asked.

'I've been working on a scenario that the killer did know the gun was there and planned it. Doesn't work any too well,' Locker said. He regarded Bone until he got a nod, and went on. 'The shot that killed Hervey was from Cryer's gun, so the murder was likely unprepared unless the killer knew it was there. So, put it that he did, had picked the locks to get at it and arranged a rendezvous with Hervey in that room on purpose. We've got all Cryer's household and several of his friends – list here – who knew the pistol was there, but none of them is likely to have had picklocks or easy access to them. Rees has a master key to the bedroom but not the drawer, and any of the household might know a better way to get rid of picklocks than to chuck them in a bush. None of them knew Hervey and only Mel Rees had met "Alix Hamilton" before. So unless we can establish a connection, motive's lacking.'

Sergeant Harris said, 'On the other hand, chucking the pickers in a bush is anonymous.'

Shay snorted suddenly. 'Wish you'd seen Wilkins with them coming out of the rhododendrons with these things over his ear like cherry earrings.'

'You didn't tell us that before,' Bone said. 'Wish I'd been there.'

'He'd got his sleeve caught so he couldn't get them off, and was stood there up to his chest in leaves and saying "What the bleep's this on me ear?" I've never needed a camera so bad.'

A few seconds to enjoy the picture, then Bone said, 'Let's see this list.'

'Cryer can't be sure who he told, but security is something people are interested in if they have any problems of their own, things to protect. He'd chatted to Jay Tansley-Ferrars and Prestbury. He'd consulted Sutton Somerton. Serafin knew, and "Alix Hamilton" for what it's worth.'

Fredricks said, 'Sir. Could Hamilton-Hervey have arranged a meeting that went wrong? If he-she knew the gun was there?'

'Let's not dismiss the idea. The likelihood remains that the killer was there primarily to steal the monstrance.'

'So we have a plain thief or a religious obsessive?'

'And supposing our plain thief is Mick Parsons, as does not seem beyond the bounds of possibility, he is not a likely killer. A religious obsessive might be capable of an impulsive act. Parsons is a shy and cautious lad, you tell me.'

'Could have had an accident while threatening Hervey.'

'I'd see Parsons as throwing the gun in the bushes along with the picklocks. And would he prop Hervey in the bed?'

'Prestbury, then?'

'Prestbury of that ilk is a very sly-seeming character. We have a possible Brown Brother there. A visitor told him of the ghost of a monk there earlier this year, and he was much struck by this. A monk, a brown brother. And he used one of the same phrases to us during the interview; these are tenuous, but could be significant.'

Detective-Inspector Blane arrived, heavy-eyed

and apologetic. He thought he had got the stomach bug. His sergeant was carrying a Fairy Liquid box full of objects and papers, for which Locker made room on the table.

'We've been through Hervey's house and flat, sir, and come up with items of definite interest.' Blane's manner was usually precise and when, as now, he was pleased with himself the result irritated Bone. He saw Locker's mouth furl into refusal to be impressed. 'What I thought most significant are here, but there's still written material we have not been able to go through. I thought it more important we should get here and report, and go through the rest this morning.'

He produced, in their plastic bags, a series of black objects: a pair of long boots with spike heels; a leather shirt; trousers; two whips and a dog leash; an ugly-looking helmet that covered the whole face with a zip across the mouth; a complicated black double belt heavy with studs and plaques, linked with chains.

They surveyed them for a moment. Someone whistled.

'We thought this was a kinky case at the start,' Bone remarked. 'This, we did not expect. Where were they, Blane?'

'In the false bottom of a wardrobe. At the flat. These papers were in a large manilla envelope taped to the back of the desk against the wall. The leathers don't show much signs of wear, except for the helmet – that's been sweated into heavily. The shirt or top is padded where the bust would be.'

There was also a make-up box, an empty wig

box, a packet of fishnet tights, another of stockings, unopened.

Blane, with an ineffable air of doing everyone a favour, tipped a series of glossy prints on to the table's scarred top.

'Do you want to go, Fredricks? Darbay?' Bone turned to the women present. Fredricks said, 'I've seen a victim of child abuse; that was really obscene. These men are perfectly willing.'

'It's a curious thing,' Bone observed, passing the prints on, 'that people can set up a gymnasium for people to suffer in and we think no more of it. DIY pain is benevolently regarded. It's when someone sets out to provide pain for others who are, as Pat says, perfectly willing, that we blench.'

'It's hardly the same thing, Superintendent,' Blane said. Bone raised an eyebrow at him.

'A different kind of satisfaction, you think.' Bone looked at the print he was holding, the blonde dominatrix, the kneeling man. 'What irony that the woman is a man. I don't think the "victim" would have liked that.'

'Surely in these skin-tight clothes it would have showed,' Locker said. Bone reached for the belt and held it up. The lower, wider belt with its huge buckle was slung from the hip-belt on crossed chains and straps. It might, and in one of the pictures clearly did, cover the crotch.

'Remote-control or time-switch camera,' Shay said.

Blane produced a spiral-backed cheap notebook. 'This had only one set of prints, and without close examination they seem to belong to Hervey. It's a record of money payments, with initials heading the pages, and dates of payment. I'll get the pages photocopied.'

Bone held out a hand for it.

'Some of them are really small sums, sir,' Blane said.

'But there's a lot of them,' Bone replied. '*It was a power thing. He liked manipulating.* So his cousin said. I don't think the cousin knew about this. What d'you think, Locker?'

'No. He said Hervey was short of cash; this is a nice little earner, wouldn't you say.' Locker pushed at the prints. 'It's not the sex, is it, that turns you up? I mean, there's all sorts and they're welcome to what sort of sick fun turns them on. They need psychiatry, you'd say. It's nasty, but it's consenting adults. The blackmail's another thing.'

'All part and parcel,' Blane declared.

'Were any of these men at that party?' Bone asked. 'And how do we tell if they were?'

'Wouldn't half make an interesting identity parade,' Shay muttered. Fredricks made an amused sound and coughed.

'I don't think this is in any way funny,' Blane said. 'I think it is horrific.'

'It's sad, perhaps,' Bone said. 'We're all very well-adjusted ourselves. No fantasy lives. Right, let's see the copies of the book. I think it's cleverly done if it's blackmail; a reasonable income, small sums all the time, nothing large enough for the well-heeled to mind paying; random dates and even reductions on previous payments, keeping the clients sweet.' Before handing the book back he saw the orderly initials heading the pages were not uniform. One page had only twined snakes.

'This picture's out of place,' Locker said. He had fished out a print of a small statue or figure, a mounted soldier holding a flag, regimental colours, his hand grasping the cloth against the standard to make picturesque folds, all painted in natural colours.

'This is up your street, Shay,' said Bone.

'That's right, sir. This was on that shelf in Tansley-Ferrars' house. Or one like it. A bit at the back. I'm not sure it was the same sort exactly. It had some other soldiers in front.'

'Must be something questionable about it or why's it here?' Bone leant to see it. 'Anything on the back? No. Pat, go and ask for the account-book again.'

When Pat brought it, Bone riffled through looking for T-F; but he found J. The sums were small, nothing above a tenner. He sent it back for copying and said, 'Jay Tansley-Ferrars collects these figures, or would if he could afford it. Supposition: he came by this one in a dodgy manner, and Hervey knew or found out.'

'And being a friend, he sort of kept him under an obligation. Good for the odd taxi-fare or drink or what-have-you,' Locker said. 'It's not nice.'

'What interests me is that Hervey bothered to write down every small amount; as if he wanted to keep track of what he was dunning them for.'

'Manipulation,' said Locker, glumly disapproving. 'Power. Like tweaking a tail. They've got to stand for this when I choose!'

'Doesn't put Tansley-F. in the prime suspects list. The standard-bearer must have been nicked from another collector, but why? Why on earth? You'd have to be a rabid collector to do that.'

'"Spare your country's flag, she said."'

'Excuse me, sir.' A PC came in with coffee. 'They've just called through that Mick Parsons has been found and they're bringing him over. An ex-girl-friend grassed, or so they think, because a woman phoned in giving an address and saying he was living there with his latest girl.'

'His latest girl. Let it be a lesson to you, Steve. If you are going to take up crime, be faithful. A cast-off girl may not take it nicely, *nor hell a fury like a woman scorned*.'

'I'll keep that well in mind,' said Locker. 'Though even without turning to crime, I think Cherry might not care for any how's-your-father on the side. She might get very shirty. She always wants to know if there's any pretty girl on any case I'm on.'

'I hope you told her about Mary Highmountain,' Bone said. As Parsons was brought into the office they were using, Bone thought immediately of the 'tall person' seen across Cryer's rooms. Mick Parsons gangled in as though he had always found his height a disadvantage when he needed to go unseen. City-pale, with quick eyes in rather swollen lids, and a long nose, he had an alarmingly wide and mobile mouth whose thin top lip rose into a curl at the ends. It made him look as if he found life wryly funny despite the way it used him. He had lank thick dark hair that he pushed back, now and then, with restless fingers.

135

'What's this about, then? I mean of course I want to be helpful but what can I tell you you don't know already? I was at Cryer's but I had to leave early; this is the first I've heard that going to parties is wrong. I didn't know anyone was dead until your fellows told me this morning.' He spoke rapidly, aggrieved.

'Didn't you really?' Locker asked. 'Not though you were in the bathroom next to it all?'

The dark eyes flickered, from Locker to Bone to Locker again. 'Me? Look, squire, I've got form, who's denying it? But you're not fixing me for this, no way.' He smiled widely with anxiety. 'It's easy, I can see that, saves trouble all round, there's our old friend Mick Parsons on the list, he'll do.'

'Who's fixing anything on you?' Locker demanded. 'I'll start thinking you have a naughty conscience. What we have got, to keep everything above-board and on record, is your print on the wc seat.'

Parsons fixed his gaze on Locker and sucked his lips.

'What seat? What wc seat? Can't anyone take a tinkle?'

'Seat in Cryer's bathroom, Mick. His private bathroom. Kept so spick and span by his staff that there was only one print, we didn't need to compare with any of the rest we took; we just lifted it, sent it in, and they tell us it's you.'

Again the eyes did their survey. Then Parsons raised his hands and dropped them. His voice too had dropped its challenge. 'No arguing with that.' He waited, looking more slowly from Locker to the silent Bone, wary, streetwise rather than clever. As neither spoke he grinned again, tentatively, and said, 'I was in the bathroom, right? Lifted the seat, right? You wouldn't want me to mess it?'

'Stop poncing around,' Locker said sharply. 'You're in trouble, Parsons. Someone's been shot.'

'I tell you I didn't know. Left before anything happened.'

'We know what time you left.'

'You can't nail me for it. I'll tell you. I'm here to tell you, right? I'll tell you the lot.'

'So tell us,' Bone said. Parsons swivelled his eyes, then his attention, and spoke to Bone.

'Well – I went in that bedroom on the off chance, see what I could see.'

Bone sat back. He said to Locker, exasperated in tone, 'Forget it. This one's going to play silly buggers all day. Charge him as accessory, put him away to cool off.'

'What've I said?' Parsons cried, flinging out his hands. 'I'm going to tell you.'

'Then start at the beginning, man,' Bone said, loud and forceful. 'The door was locked. You could have gone anywhere in the house but you went to Cryer's bedroom, which was locked. What were you looking for?'

'There'd be nothing worth my notice anywhere that was open, would there? Stands to reason what's valuable is going to be in somewhere that's locked.'

'When I went round the house,' Bone said, in a voice at the edge of patience, 'there were dozens of small objects worth money. You left them. You went for the bedroom. Parsons, I'm offering you a chance. You knew what you were looking for and you knew where it was. Picklocks were found in the garden, of all the bloody silly places to chuck them. Now.'

'Well, I panicked. I panicked, right? Look I'll *start* at the beginning. I'm doing my best. I got a tip there was something worth having in that bedroom and I got in there, right?'

'What were you looking for? What was this "something worth having"? *Exactly*?'

'Well, it's a large article of jewellery.'

'How large?'

Mick's long hands indicated. 'It was there on the chest, large as life, shape of a sun and all over gemstones, as per description.'

'A monstrance, Mick. An article of church furniture. This is a picture of it.'

'That's right.' Mick leant to look and smiled brightly.

'Where did you plan to sell this highly identifiable piece?'

'Sell it? There's a dozen places—'

Bone stood up. Locker, following the signal, gathered papers and tapped them on the desk to align them. He said, 'Michael Gary Parsons—'

'No, no. Christ. Listen. *Listen*. This geezer wanted the thing, the monsterance. He said if I got it there was a thou in it for me.'

Bone sat down.

'Why did you monkey around if you know all that?' Parsons demanded pathetically.

138

'To coin a phrase, *we're* asking the questions,' said Locker. 'Why did you open the bedside table drawer if you were looking for the monstrance which was in plain sight?'

'Well, it's the off chance, isn't it? People keep all sorts by their beds. Could of been something really useful.'

'You saw the gun?'

'Course I saw it. No use to me, was it? I hate the things. Genuine. Never carried one, wouldn't touch them. Who wants trouble?' Parsons' answers were littered with questions, but now he came out with a real one. 'Can I smoke, Super? I'm on edge. Nerves aren't good at the best.'

Bone gestured permission, forebore comment. He and Cherry Locker had got Steve to stop two years ago, and he had plenty of ammunition on the subject. Parsons lit up, inhaled a full quarter of the cigarette at one go, and breathed out, slowly, turning his head aside in delicate consideration.

'In fact seeing the shooter put me off. I'd have locked it; I mean I'm not careless. Only someone was coming – there's no carpet outside – and they stopped and I nipped in the bathroom. I'm all nerves, and when they tried the bedroom door and came in I never felt more like a pee. Until later that is. I slipped the bolt. Hoped it wasn't Cryer and if it was he didn't need a pee. Then I made out it was high heels. Then I heard this voice, well, two voices, there was a man talking and a woman, and the woman sounded pissed, giggling and dancing around. Sometimes it sounded like a man was there and then not. I never heard his feet. Then someone else come in, a squeak like it could be rubber shoes, right? And footsteps all right, and a different voice, and I thought, there's three of them. By this time I was crossing my legs, I tell you. It's funny now, I mean, right?' His glance at the two of them did not give him support for this idea and he went on, subdued. 'But anyway this new bloke says something, like, angry or, I dunno, but there was a bit of hassle, feet stamping around, you know? But it wasn't that easy to hear because of all the racket downstairs. Voices I could hear because they had to shout or speak up anyways but they came quite near the door, and this bloke was talking through his teeth, really mad and the woman was laughing. And then the curtain rings make a noise, and a bit of quiet and then it starts up again, more talk and argy-bargy, it sounded like the woman was leading him on. I thought I hope they do it quick and get out. She was laughing away, and calling out like she was teasing, that sort of wouldn't-you-like-some, and then a shot. Nearly hit the ceiling, I did. I mean, I near as a touch wet myself. I thought, the way you do, they'll shoot the lock off and come and get me. I mean, you see films about it all the time, right?'

Bone reflected that Mick did not seem to have connected the shot with anyone else's danger but his own.

'I waited on and there was quiet. I thought, they've all gone. And I risked it, I had to, I was in agony, I took a Jimmy. I listened all right, but the music was on and I reckoned nobody heard, anyway nobody came trying the door. So I came out. You can bet I was dead curious, right? But I couldn't believe it! There was this girl, I'd fancied her earlier on, she was really – you know? – all *right* – lying, sort of sitting up lying back easy, on all the pillows and looking across the room. I sort of ducked back. There was still this heavy beat stuff from downstairs and it was really getting to my stomach, you know? I looked out again and she didn't move. Christ, I mean, spooky. It was spooky. She just didn't move. Well, I did, I can tell you. I thought, I could be here for ever, so I risked it. I was out of there like the Hound of the Baskervilles, I didn't wait, you can stand on that.'

'Except for the monstrance.'

Mick went blank. 'What do you mean? I scarpered, I tell you. I'd heard shooting, right? And I didn't know why the whole party wasn't coming up to know what gives. And there was her staring in the bed with her hair and the dress. I just went. I didn't wait for the whatsit. I'd forgot it. When I got to the stairs I stopped and breathed. Like I don't think I breathed from when I saw her until then. So what did I do? There was a window open and I leant out and I thought maybe I'd climb out and go, but then I thought of all the security and the big fence and that, so I just took the wires and threw them far as they'd go into the bushes. And I went down and got a drink. I never needed a drink more. I got a lot of drinks. I had to throw up off the motorway, Gwyn was really mad. He said the hard shoulder's not safe, they run into you. He wouldn't speak for miles. But what could I tell him? Soon as we got back to his place I said goodbye and got lost. And now I told you every-thing. I really have. I'm clean.'

'You are?'

Mick's alarm widened his eyes. 'What you want? You can't try anything. I'm clean.'

'Are you? Who tipped you about the monstrance? Who was going to pay you that thou?'

Parsons went back to looking shifty, and got out his cigarettes. Bone got up, and he paused, holding the packet, watched him come round the desk, take the packet from his hand and lay it on the blotter.

'Where's the monstrance, Parsons? Someone wanted it.'

Parsons gripped the sides of his chair like a child. 'No,' he said. 'You got to be joking. Go back past her? I mean later on I was kicking myself. There was a thousand nicker sitting there and I'd spent time arsing round looking for what else; and then I'd run. You could of got it, I thought after. But I didn't. I went out of there like the clappers and I wasn't going back in. I mean old whoosit could whistle for his church thing. He could bloody get it for himself and I'd've told him if I'd seen him but—'

Mick's jaw wavered, he gave Bone a flat stare, took breath deeply and said, 'But I haven't seen him to tell him.'

Bone took a long shot not quite in the dark. 'He'd left the party, then?'

'Christ you know all of it. What are you leading me on for? *Give* us a fag.'

Bone slid the pack across. They waited while Parsons lit up. His hands were shaking.

'He wanted it for religious reasons,' he said,

142

putting his lighter away. 'He said I needn't think he wanted it for anything criminal. This monster'd been nicked out of a church in the first place and he wanted to give it back there. Cryer'd be just as happy with the insurance money and so on and so on. I knew it was a scam, I mean there's nothing legit about a deal like that, but he wanted to be all right with himself, didn't he?' He drew deeply once more. Then logic got through to him. 'You mean the monster's missing.'

Bone maintained a repressive silence. Parsons almost missed his mouth with the cigarette and then dragged on it.

'I haven't got it. I didn't take it. If it's gone I'm not to blame. Maybe he got the nerve together to walk in and help himself. I don't know. I *don't* know, God help me I don't. And I never touched the gun. I'm a bleeding amateur in all this; I didn't lock the door, I even took my glove off for a pee.' He was angrily grieved. 'Look, I didn't even know if she was dead. I just ran. I don't know why nobody heard the shot. It made a bloody great crack.' He finished the cigarette down to the butt and stubbed it on his shoe-sole. 'I just ran,' he repeated.

Bone in his mind's eye saw this ungainly great bat out of hell leaving Cryer's room.

'The name, Mick. The name. Who hired you?'

'Oh, Christ. I mean you're not going to even believe me.'

'Try.'

'He's called Prestbury.' He tossed the butt into the wastebin. He sagged in the chair. The PC by the door watched him with resigned indifference. There was a shrill parental voice from the car park beneath the windows, and a whine of childen. Nothing in Bone's face showed his satisfaction at having a theory confirmed. He said, 'We could try another story. Suppose you'd been hired to set up something different. To open up Cryer's room, and the gun drawer, for someone.'

Parsons, his face a mask of dismay, was on his feet. Locker and the PC converged. He sat down before they touched him. 'I never. Look, this Prestbury. Ask him. He's the bleeding magistrate.'

'He's going to laugh,' Locker said.

'He can laugh till he shits, he *did* it, he called me up and said he had a job of work for me, and I borrowed some wheels off of Gwyn Griffiths and I went, I got to this horrible house and he gave me a zonking pink gin and did his talk about the whatsit.'

'Monstrance.' It was surprising the difficulty caused even to Locker by this unfamiliar word. It stumped Shay and now Parsons, who was unwilling to try it as evinced by his, 'Yeh well. So for a G it seemed worth it. And I could get to Cryer's with Gwyn if I pushed it a bit. Gwyn's a softie except when he's at work.'

'How did Prestbury know you could get into Cryer's? Did he expect that you would break in?'

'He knew I belonged with the crowd. We were shooting Cryer's video for *Doesn't Grow on Trees* there, weren't we? At Prestbury's. There's this big derelict sort of garden all walled round Cryer took a fancy to and Prestbury let him make the video there. Well I say *let him* but of course Cryer'd pay, wouldn't he? When I saw the old gasbag strutting about I kept out of his way all right, but he saw me, and I saw him talk to Gwyn right after. I wasn't that worried, because Gwyn knew I had form, right? But Cryer didn't. It's a great video. You seen it? No, well, but Cryer's ever so fantastically clever. He asked Prestbury to his house because old Prestbury took some of them round his own horrible great dump. I reckon Prestbury would've seen the gismo then, don't you think? Prestbury's that much of a prat he's even called his house after himself.' Parsons had talked his way into a degree of confidence. He looked up almost brightly with this evidence of Prestbury's pomposity.

'I'm not fully satisfied,' Bone said. 'However, you'll be charged with entering with intent to steal.' He nodded to Locker, delivering this long stringy pigeon into his hands, and went out to see what was happening. Harris gave him the news that Dr Monro Walsh, still suffering from concussion after his car crash the night of the party, was recovering and might shortly be in a position to talk. It was unlikely that he had seen anything and not spoken to Cryer of it, but he had been visiting Jeremy on the same landing at approximately the time of the murder. He might have heard the shot.

Bone's maverick imagination presented him with a vignette of Dr Walsh, enraged with sudden passion for Alix Hamilton, making her a histrionic proposition and, repulsed, shooting her dead. The car crash was clearly an expression of remorse.

He entertained this idea enough to consider that the shooting had been done with one bullet, whereas a wild passion might require the expenditure of the whole clip. Lamia Hervey had been surprised, when she tried to shoot again, that her husband's automatic had only the single shot left; her state of mind had required that she shoot again and again. The use of one bullet suggested coolness, but did not guarantee it. Parsons had heard argument, and the shouting might be an effort to be heard above the amplifiers rather than violence of temper.

But then, shouting had a kick-back effect: it produced temper.

Prestbury, he thought. That odd, devious glance. Prestbury was not likely to remain on the Bench after this came out. Bone heard Locker say he would be going to bring Prestbury in. Conspiracy to steal. What had possessed the man? It couldn't be called religion, except in the way that men make religion an excuse for any of the seven deadly sins. It wasn't for God that Prestbury wanted the monstrance.

People were going to lunch; a good idea. Bone thought of the Swan. Charlotte's school would have had their break-up ceremony by now and she would be at Prue's. He need not telephone as he would if she were at home alone. He would have a pub lunch.

CHAPTER NINE

As he walked down the street he milled the facts over. Suppose Parsons to be telling the truth, where had the monstrance got to? Patience did not appear to be one of Prestbury's characteristics and it might be that he had come upstairs and got it himself. Had he got it while Alix was alive or when she was dead? Would Parsons not have known his voice if he had come in and argued with her? Would Parsons now be shielding him if he thought him a killer?

Parsons, Bone estimated, would nervously shop his own mother if the going got tough.

The Case of the Missing Monstrance? he said to himself. Do we believe Mick Parsons. Where would he have stashed the thing, had he got it? Was it at Prestbury in the the chapel already? Bone thought of telling the Chief he wanted a warrant to search a magistrate's house.

Of course! Do a deal with Parsons, he thought flippantly, to break into the chapel and see.

Murder before monstrance, he said, after this excursion into the bizarre. First the murderer, then the thief. The two might or might not be the same. They might or might not be connected.

He paused, realizing he had walked on too far, and looked across the road. The car tucked against

Emily Playfair's hedge, the green Mini, wasn't it Grizel Shaw's? Bone at once decided he ought to make enquiries about Alex Hervey's cat; find out how he had settled and whether he were being troublesome. With a sense of heightened life, he advanced up the brick path, watched from inside a window by a thoughtful chinchilla, and pressed the bell.

Mrs Playfair opened the door wide. She was in blue that made her eyes more blue than ever, and she welcomed him with a delighted cry. 'Robert! Splendid.' Taking a pinch of his sleeve she drew him in. 'Go on. Front room.'

He went in, and his scanning glance at once came to rest. Grizel Shaw, sprawled elegantly on the floor in a loose green teeshirt and lemon and green check cotton trousers, was trailing a length of string under the chintz skirts of an armchair. She looked up at him, the sunlight in her wide, cat's eyes so that their pupils were small. She smiled slowly, while a disturbance took place under the chair and a kitten came rolling out with the string over one ear.

She stood up, bringing the kitten in one hand. After a moment she said, 'I asked Charlotte where she got Ziggy, so here I am cat-hunting.'

'Oh yes,' Bone said, brilliantly improvising.

'I'm so glad you're here,' Emily said. 'You're nicely in time for lunch.'

'I certainly can't,' he said, turning, reluctant. 'After yesterday it would –'

'Be absolutely necessary. I probably knew you were coming, because I made an immense *daube*.

And not only is feeding the police a *public duty* which you have no right to deny me, but also it will help to save Mameluke from a coronary, since he always tries to cope with the left-overs. Good!' and she made for the kitchen at a fast trot.

The teeshirt had slipped to the corner of Grizel's left shoulder, disclosing a smooth slope from the neck with no straps. She caressed the kitten. 'I thought I had best look for a wee cat quickly, so I could get it used to the house while I was there in the holidays. As you might say, break it in. Mrs Playfair said there were kittens almost ready now. What do you think of this one?'

Held up in her slender hand, the kitten peered about. It was a chinchilla cross, with a good helping of tabby. Bone put up a finger to support its chill paw.

'It's charming.'

'The trouble is that there are four of them.'

'Yes,' he said. Her presence made him curiously happy, and with an effort he stirred his mind to make sense of what she had said. 'Cha chose the one that seemed to like her.'

He wanted to turn that into some compliment about all the kittens being bound to like her, but the artificiality of it kept him silent.

'That's a good idea. Provided that any of them do.'

'They might all,' he said.

She laughed; and the kitten now beginning to semaphore a wish to be on the ground, she bent. The ridge of her spine showed between the loose green and the fitting yellow-and-green. She straightened up and said, 'I must help Mrs Play-fair.' She stood, however, where she was, her clear green eyes nearly level with his.

'You haven't been here before, then?'

'No. Isn't it a lovely house?'

Bone thought he had said 'charming' recently and said 'Indeed it is.' He looked about, desperate at being devoid of speech, a cliché in itself. 'Rich in cats.'

'Yes! If I could cope with them I'd want as many myself. Mrs Playfair says she'll show me all of them. Do you know how many there are?'

'When I first met her there were fifteen. Last time Cha and I were over here it was nine, but more expected.'

'That will be Daisy's four, I dare say.'

'Very likely; which suggests there are now thirteen.'

Emily Playfair came in, not down the brick steps from the kitchen, but down the hall with a serving trolley. The floors at the back of the house sloped so much that she had a ready-made ramp along the hall. 'We were wondering how many cats there are here,' Grizel said, going forward to help.

'Fourteen. That is, thirteen and a boarder.'

Bone remembered Tombola. 'That's my fault. I dumped a homeless cat on Mrs Playfair yes-terday.'

'My name is Emily,' said Mrs Playfair severely, and softened it with her triangular, dimpled smile. She and Grizel opened the gate-legged table to its full oval, and she set mats and silver, a plate

150

of cheese, a biscuit box, a green glass bowl of apples and oranges. The sleek Arletty jumped on a chair to survey this. Emily put a lid over the cheese.

'Last time I made a *daube*, that one was in trouble,' and she nodded at Arletty. 'I took out the *bouquet garni* and laid it on the side, and she ate it. Whether it was the gravy on it, or the herbs, I don't know. I caught her at it just in time to draw it out by the string. You have to do that very carefully. This svelte young creature, Mrs Shaw, is a glutton. She will eat anything and never the worse for it – except for string, which I can't risk; and the bay leaf. I've put the *bouquet* right away this time.'

The *daube* smelt rich and dark. Bone received his blue plate with the meat, the bacon, the gravy, the small mushrooms and little onions. The three people at table were surrounded by an outer ring of cats – Daisy, Arletty, Big Dorrit, the vast Mameluke, sunk in his rusty cloud of black, and a grey tabby whose name Bone had forgotten. Was it Miss Flite?

'I hear Dr Walsh is improving,' Bone said. 'He's your doctor, isn't he?'

'No, I go to Dr Bellrose, I get on better with her. Dr Walsh is impatient with cats, something of a disadvantage in this household. Poor Marian Wheatley, you heard she'd slipped and fallen? She's taken to midnight snacking in her seventies, and she was raiding the fridge. It is my belief that the daughter-in-law keeps her short, with the best of motives, but if an old woman mayn't gluttonize, what pleasure is left? But she took a fall, and at her age there's always the risk of a broken hip, so they rang Dr Walsh, and his emergency service passed the message to the Manor. Marian said he was in quite a paddy when he arrived, telling her about drunks in the road. I'll put Arletty out, Robert. She has no discretion.'

'I really don't mind.'

'One can't eat with a cat walking on one's lap,' said Emily, dropping Arletty with a soft thud inside the kitchen and shutting the door, 'however nice one is. So ironic that the poor doctor was complaining of drunks when it was one of them who drove into him not an hour later. Marian did not feel very bad, and she was afraid he was angry with her for calling him out. Not that she did, it was young Bill. But Dr Walsh sat there and flung open his case, she said, to get out his blood pressure thing, and he stared and then swore. She was surprised because he's much against swearing, and she supposed he must have forgotten something, or brought the *wrong* things. You see, once he had a box of chocolates given him by a grateful patient, and he really is a tireless doctor, I may tell you; and he got so cross tugging his stethoscope out from under that box that it suddenly rained chocolates all over the counterpane. Marian said that she kept finding them later, much better than aspirins. But there were no chocolates this time, so although she asked, she never found out what it was.'

Grizel ate neatly, in no hurry, listening.

'It seems a great shame that someone like Dr

Walsh should get run into like that. Still, the drunk young man from Rolvenden has broken his arm and his nose, they say, which may make him more careful.'

Grizel's kitten here fell backwards off the window-sill with great nonchalance, and walked across to Daisy shaking its ears.

'I've temporarily called that one Houdini,' Emily said.

Bone, still apt to turn cold at talk of drunken drivers, caught Grizel's eye as she turned from the sight of Daisy holding down Houdini to wash him. They smiled.

For a moment Emily was silent. When Bone glanced at her, she was regarding her plate, and the dimple in her cheek showed as if she also had been smiling.

'I'd ask you about your work, Robert, only one isn't supposed to. Tombola is an affectionate cat but he's been neglected. I suppose his owner was always very busy. Poor man, what an end to come to.'

'I thought it was a woman,' said Grizel, 'if you mean at the Manor.'

Emily Playfair looked vague. 'Was it? I thought, a man. Now there's cheese, and biscuits, and fruit. No, I'll just take the casserole out and put the coffee on. You can't help, bless you. What guests are coming to! They won't stay put.'

Her eyes twinkled as she withdrew, pulling the trolley.

Grizel said in a low voice, 'Cha told me Mrs Playfair was a super person. One has to allow for

153

teenage understatement. I am very glad to have met her.'

'You don't live far from here.' Bone made, as so often he did, a question that could be a statement.

'No. In Adlingsden. And I endorse every word of praise of Dr Walsh. He's very, very good at his job. When I finally got my divorce from Lewis, and was expecting life to take an upward turn from then on, I had a breakdown instead. I didn't know what was happening to me, but I thought a tonic would do no harm, or perhaps I needed a blood test and some treatment; so along I went to this Monro Walsh because he was recommended to me. I told him it was very likely a vitamin shortage. He gave me the most gloomy stare you can imagine, and said, "Of course you could have vitamins, but there are better things to do with your money. You need to eat better and to pamper yourself for a while." I burst into tears. He was kindness itself, but you could never get to know him. He usually looks as if he's going to say something scathing. And sometimes he does, too, but he's just as likely to come out with something kind and apt.'

'A good man,' Emily said, sitting down, 'though I would not add, a tolerant one.'

'He's what they nowadays call "caring",' Grizel said. She gave the dish of cheeses to Bone, and their eyes held for a moment before they managed to look away. He thought *this is absurd*, and he felt a ridiculous bubble of happiness.

Arletty had come in after Emily, and she now combed past Grizel's chair. Looking down, Grizel cried, 'She's done it again!' and she picked the cat up. From the side of the furry lips hung a thread of cotton string, soggy with gravy, and Arletty was delicately gagging. Emily and Bone sprang up and converged. He helped to hold the graceful, affronted creature, his hands over Grizel's and her head next to his face, her pale short hair brushing his cheek. Emily took the string and gradually, softly drew it out. Arletty retched, hissed, complained, and produced the whole thread, knotted but without its herbs. Emily exclaimed about the bayleaf, blaming herself furiously, when on cue Arletty's slender body started to heave. Emily whipped a newspaper from the side table, Grizel held the cat on it despite her tendency to walk backwards onto the carpet as she brought up an unlovely little macédoine.

'There's the bayleaf,' Grizel said, pointing with professional finger. 'She's rid of it.'

'She must have torn open the plastic bag I'd tied it in. Arletty, you are the daughter of a goat.'

Bone, reluctantly moving away from the smell of Grizel's skin, watched Arletty stalk away and sit down to wash.

Emily, bundling up newspaper, said, 'What were we talking about? I hope that hasn't put you off. I'll bring coffee.'

'We were talking about poor Dr Walsh, I believe.'

'You know, he doesn't seem to be lucky with that medical case. I'm told that in the crash it shot out of the door and spilt all over the grass verge and the hedge. Poor Berryman had to search the whole area for bits and pieces, and he didn't even know what he was looking for.'

She stopped in the kitchen door and said in a different tone, 'What is that round thing in the ditch? The thing like a sun?'

'The sun in the ditch?' asked Grizel. She saw Bone's face. 'It's a clue!' She turned round towards him. He said, 'It's a lead. But in the ditch?'

Emily stood on the brick step leading to the kitchen, giving her head a little shake like a cat whose fur has been rumpled. 'Dear me. What was that?'

'It sounds as if it could be the monstrance,' Bone said incautiously, rising. 'I'd better send Berryman back there to have a wider hunt.'

'Oh, can't we go and look?' Grizel cried. Bone, ever too inclined to move about and see things for himself, met her excited eyes and broke into a smile.

'Why should Berryman have the fun? I'll bring my car and – exactly where did Walsh's accident happen, Mrs – Emily?'

'At the bend just this side of the Rolvenden turning, so they say.' She was smiling now. 'A monstrance? Yes, I expect it is.'

'I know the place you mean,' Grizel said, 'and I've got my car here. Let's go.'

'Oh do,' Emily urged. 'But tell me about it, mind. Telephone when you get home. And about the kitten, you have first choice of the litter and can decide any time.' She came with them towards the door; Grizel picked a green leather shoulder-bag from an armchair on the way. 'You can try Charlotte's test: see which of them likes *you* best.'

156

'But they all might,' Bone repeated. Emily tapped his arm, her glance sparkling approval, while Grizel laughed. They said their goodbyes, and she ran down the brick path, Bone hurrying after. He felt lighthearted, almost effervescent in spirits, hardly his usual mood on a case.

He folded himself into the pasenger seat and snapped the belt. She said, 'You'll need more leg room,' and showed him how he could move back. He said, 'I'm all right,' not wanting to sit further back. 'Am I in your way, though?'

'I've not changed gears with anyone's knees in a long while. We'll go round by Padgett's Corner.'

Bone was relieved but not surprised that she drove well. Petra had been a very careful driver, sometimes making him impatient. Alison and her husband were both erratic drivers, harsh on gears, but he felt safe and at ease in Grizel's car, sitting so that he could watch her profile, close enough to see the gold down on her cheek.

'Now, a monstrance – It's a religious thing, isn't it? For holding the Eucharist?'

'Yes.'

'And you've mislaid one.'

'Yes.'

'And Emily – you seemed to know what was going on, but I'm not sure I do. She said it was in the ditch.'

'I forgot that you wouldn't know. Emily has second sight. I don't much – I tend not to believe in these things; or to be sceptical. There've been cases, though, and I'm quite convinced about Emily. The first time I met her she knew something about the

157

case we hadn't given out to the public; and she's done it again.' He did not mention Emily's thinking the victim was a man, both because it was not being divulged yet, and because he was not sure he hadn't implied as much to Emily when he brought Tombola. 'So when she saw the sun in the ditch, I thought at once . . .'

He was silent as she negotiated a turn past road works.

'And you've mislaid a monstrance; or someone has.'

'It's missing. If this is it, I'm entirely at a loss how Walsh came to have it.' Bone, fleetingly aware that he was indeed talking about the case to a member of the public, dismissed the thought. 'It's not surprising that he could have got it. He was visiting Cryer's son who was ill. I don't understand the rest. It upsets every scenario so far.' This appealed to him at the moment as stimulating.

'But who had it in the first place?'

'Ken Cryer. He collects things that interest him, things in the style of the Manor, I suppose.' He watched her neat, tough hands on the wheel. She had no wedding ring; probably shed it at the time of the divorce. She had 'expected life to take an upward turn' once she was free of her husband. There were so many ways for a marriage to go rotten, and he wished Grizel had not had to find any of them. Was it perhaps better to lose a partner by an abrupt severance than by the decay of love?

I am even feeling protective, he thought.

'Some of the girls could talk about nothing else this morning but Ken Cryer and Archangel. Charlotte's autograph brought half the school in for a stare while we were supposed to be clearing up the Biology Room.'

'Oh yes. He's a nice man – they both are. Cryer's lifestyle is less flamboyant than Serafin's. Mind you, I don't know Serafin at all. I've been to dinner at Cryer's, so I know him a little. Serafin's another thing.'

'Hyper-glitzy, I'm informed. The girls read all the magazines and gossip columns.' She looked sidelong, and they laughed. Suddenly he laughed again.

'Do you know I've committed a major sin?'

'You have?'

'I didn't tell a soul where I was going! I hope there's a phone box along here. It's a major sin that any of my team would be on the carpet for.'

'Then they'll be a bit pleased that you've committed it, no doubt. People like their superiors to be fallible. It suggests that, after all, they're human.'

'I'm not sure that's a good thing,' he said. They were at cross-roads, and he fell silent while she made a 225° turn into a narrow lane. He thought: I'm human. With this woman I'm like a boy with a girl. It's been years since this happened.

'It's about here,' she said, slowing. 'Yes, look.' The verge was rutted, the road surface held the skid marks and discolouration where debris had been swept up. The stems of grasses were crowded with fragments of rust, dried earth, plastic and glass. She pulled up beyond this, on a clear stretch of road, and they walked back, she on the grass verge.

'Do you really think it's here?'

'I'm prepared to find that it is.'

'It's only just struck me how quick you were to believe Emily. At the time, I was really going along without understanding it, believing because you did.'

'She says she catches things from me, that I set her off. She read somewhere that certain people have magnetic fields that affect clairvoyants, and she believes that I do, which I must say I baulk at.'

'But why?' she asked, and slithered incontinently into the ditch with a loud sharp gasp and flailing arms. Bone, clambering over the hummocky bank from the road, cried, 'Are you all right?' and she raised a rueful, smiling face.

'Are you all right?' he repeated, disproportionately anxious.

'Oh yes. Nothing traction won't cure.' She rubbed her back, grimacing. 'Now I'm down here I'd best start searching, hadn't I? It's perfectly dry, thank the Lord.'

'It seems to have more weeds than are necessary.'

'I don't think a weed would agree with you. Who are we to decide? I'll watch out for the anti-personnel kind.'

'I'd better start at the far end and work towards you,' he said, with no enthusiasm for going solo, but practically, and she said, 'No, suppose you go a few yards ahead and when I reach where you've searched, I'll go on a few yards. Leapfrog fashion.'

This seemed companionable, and he lowered himself the short distance into overgrown ditch. Under his feet was a decent basis of sand and stones. The ditch had been properly maintained and was a runnel only in rainy weather. He began to delve in the long grass, cow parsley and horse-tail, sorrel and to him innominate weeds. There was a kind absence of nettles but the occasional briar or thorn sapling. The wind, almost intangible down here, carried meringue blobs of cumulus over the stretch of sky, and their work went on in sun and shadow.

'Here's a pill bottle,' she said. 'I'll pop it in my pocket for now.'

'I've an empty half of whisky, very old. Not Walsh's.'

Bone parted the growth that hid his footing. There were no signs of Berryman's feet. He must have searched from above, as Bone had contemplated doing. Berryman had not been searching for evidence, but only to do Dr Walsh a favour and make sure that no noxious substances were lying loose. Small ferreting noises came from her. He looked back. Her cropped head, bent, turned from side to side as she probed.

'You're nearly where I began.'

She raised her head. 'So I am. Just two feet more.' He had spoken to make her look at him.

From the time two feet took her, she was being very thorough. Bone combed the hollows, the bases of plants, the foliage, to the top of the banks both sides of him, as far as the roots of hedge on his right. Hearing her scramble out, he turned.

She was agile, and passed him on the road at a trot, chose her next stint and inserted her feet with caution.

'Not quite so dry here. There must be a spring around. But not wet.'

He had to keep his attention on the searching and not on her back, on the bare waist and the riding-up teeshirt and neat rump proceeding slowly away from him. He found a propelling pencil and a prescription form, an old cigarette pack, part of a crisp packet, a bottle cap, and a belligerent thistle. He was sucking his finger as he reached where she had started.

The second time she passed him she did it at an exaggerated circus trot, and he laughed.

'The ditch is shallower here,' she reported. 'It's also full of buttercup suckers woven every which way. I need scissors.'

'Sorry.'

'I don't think the pair in my first aid box'd do.'

'You carry first aid too?'

'I got it for field trips. It's going to come in useful when we're through. I'm all over wee scratches. I suppose you carry a professional box – hey!'

She stood upright, holding something, and turned. As he made his way along, she held out both hands. Earth-stained, grass cut, they supported a golden irregular disc, with a crystal centre over an empty circle whose gold back was imprinted with IHS. From this centre spread irregular gold rays inset with small bright stones, the soft pink of ruby, the light clear green of emerald, sapphire of blue fire, and the grey-white glint of table-cut diamond. They stood looking.

'It's quite heavy,' she said. 'There must be a deal of gold. Is it not strange about precious things, that they carry a feeling with them?'

She turned it over, carefully. One of the longer rays had earth on its tip, where it had been embedded. The back, plain damascening in a ferny pattern, stood away from the front, and between them at the base was a socket for a carrying rod.

'There's not a stone missing, is there? They've been well set. There, you must have it. What do you suppose Dr Walsh was doing with the thing? He's not a thief.'

'I cannot begin to imagine,' he said.

CHAPTER TEN

'Cryer's glad to hear it's found,' Bone said to Locker, 'and we have another suspect. Opportunity; he was seeing Jem on the same landing a few doors away.'

'Motive?'

Bone, leaning an arm on the desk, pushed the end of a pencil against the faint afternoon roughness of his chin.

'He can be aggressive. Remember he tore down that girl's little shrine. And that was from religious motives. There may be a religious connection. All the same, he's a doctor and, according to various reports, a good one and concerned with saving life. Is he going to switch to murder? Say it's less possible with him than with some others, perhaps.'

'Sir,' said Berryman, and went on as Bone turned to him. 'Dr Walsh was very hot about saving life. He's very much against abortion, for instance. I know the sudden impulse can be all it takes to lead to murder, but as you say, with him being so much against abortion – my wife could tell you. She was in the waiting-room when Mr Hazeley – that's an estate agent with a big business in Tunbridge Wells but he lives locally, house called Trimms out towards Sandhurst – he came in and took the next turn ahead of everyone and they could hear him fairly yelling at the doctor. He got as good as he gave, the wife says, but everyone could hear. Hazeley was saying the doctor had no right to refuse to refer his daughter for an abortion. My wife said, you'd think he'd keep it quiet, seeing his daughter's not married, but he didn't seem to care who heard. Dr Walsh said she could go elsewhere to those who'd do what she wanted, but he would not. Life is holy, he said, and he was dedicated to saving it and he would not be responsible for ending it, not in any way. He said if Hazeley had taken proper loving care of his daughter he would not be asking such things now. All the waiting-room was drinking it in, and when Mr Hazeley came out old Gifford stuck his stick out and made him stumble. Mrs Berryman says everyone was very indignant on behalf of Dr Walsh.'

'A useful character reference, yes.'

Locker said, 'Walsh left the same time as Serafin. He'd had a call passed from his answering service: Miss Marsh gave it him when he came downstairs, to go to Mrs Wheatley in Saxhurst here, who'd had a fall.'

'I remember,' Bone said.

'Cryer told me the doctor left in a hurry. He thought it might be he was huffed at Cryer paying attention to Serafin leaving and not to him, the doctor's a bit like that.'

'He looks a bit more like a villain than a doctor, sir. He's a dark man, pale skin, and he looks grim. Very serious expression and deepset eyes.

165

There's a lot of sympathy locally about his crash. He's a very popular doctor.'

'Thank you. Well, he must have gone into Cryer's room after Mick Parsons got the door open, so he was in the room when Mick had taken refuge – in the bathroom. Steve, look up Parsons' story, would you, check what he says he heard.'

Locker referred to the print-out the office manager had sent in. 'At first Parsons doesn't know how many people are there, because he can hear a man and a woman, but he thought he'd heard high heels. Then a squeak like rubber soles, and a different voice angry, a bit of hassle, trampling feet, a man "talking through his teeth, really mad" then silence, and the woman giggling. Then curtain rings make a noise—'

'Which suggests this is when she gets, or is put, into the bed; but was still alive.'

'—and then after a moment more talk and argy-bargy, the woman leading him on, teasing. Then the shot. Then when there's been quiet, Parsons uses the toilet and makes a bolt for the door. He didn't look for the monstrance or notice anything. The woman on the bed scared him so much he got out fast. He said when I charged him he couldn't believe she was dead though he'd heard the shot. "She looked spooky, just sitting there comfortable" are his words. I checked with him about the monstrance, if he'd not seen was it or wasn't it there, but he didn't look. I needled him on it: a thousand pounds and he didn't even check. He says if she was dead there was a killer loose, if she wasn't then she could see him, and either way the shooter had been used and he wanted out.'

'Right. Then, why did Walsh take the monstrance? What did he *want* with it? Religious he may be, and incidentally he's not, someone said, Catholic but C of E?'

'Yes, sir. His daughter was confirmed along with my niece.'

'Nice to know some of the zealots are on our side,' Bone said, 'though a lot of us are C of E by default. Thank you, Berryman.'

Left alone, he went through the print-outs. All questions about the monstrance were stymied until Walsh could answer. The latest report said his daughter had arrived from Sussex University and was at his bedside talking to him in the hope of getting some reaction. Bone had sent a PC there too, a silent observer.

He could not form a scenario with Walsh storming into Cryer's room, struggling with Alix, shooting her, seizing the monstrance as if it were the Grail and packing it into his bag to sneak it from the Manor. He had, however, managed to leave without speaking to Cryer, which was significant. Leaving in a hurry might look like leaving in a huff; but was it guilt?

Was Walsh, not Prestbury, the Brown Brother? Was this a case where a popular, loved physician turned out to be helping people he disapproved of out of this world?

Cryer must be asked about Dr Walsh and the monstrance. Had the doctor disapproved of his

167

keeping the religious objects? Had he seen the monstrance before that visit?

Was Walsh perhaps connected with Alex Hervey's sinister sideline? It was a very long shot. In the photographs Hervey had kept, the men would presumably be identifiable to those who knew them well – or intimately – since either an eye-covering leather mask or a complete helmet was, apart from a dog lead, all they were wearing. There weren't many photographs. Hervey was either exclusive, or just beginning this nasty activity.

Suppose Walsh to be suffering from some condition, mental or a brain episode, that had sent him off balance, turned him kleptomaniac, even affected his driving judgement when faced with a drunk on the road?

All fantasy. Bone, however, had found his fantasies of use in the past. Not often, for most cases that were solved at all were solved by putting facts together, by forensic evidence, computer analysis, or by confession. The analysis of traces made Foster and his crew more important than ever before. *More important than I am*, Bone thought sadly, turning again to the notes on substances found on Hervey-Hamilton's dress and skin.

The adage that the murderer always left something behind and always took something away had less application when at least three people had been in the room. According to Mick it was four or five. Traces of Lamia Hervey's presence were found at the bedfoot. An automatic pistol had been fired there, traces of it and two of her hairs had been found. By the bed, more powder dust, polish from the dance floor, fingerprints of Ken, Edwina, Hervey, and faded, almost dry prints of Pak Sim, the factotum, on the table and the bedpost.

Fredricks came with the report on the monstrance, which had no recoverable prints. He had noticed how Grizel handled it between her palms, but anything on it was smeared. This did not trouble Bone, for he judged it had gone straight into Walsh's custody. All the same, he had sent it for trace analysis, of course.

Most of the gleanings from Alix Hamilton's dress matched that from Hervey's flat, some from Ken's sheet, some from make-up. On the left sleeve, matching a grip bruise, was some fabric damage and a smear of biro fluid. A note from the action allocator here: the hospital had been asked if Walsh had had biro fluid on his hand on admission. So far no answer; but they would have cleaned his hands, no doubt, and removed any traces of lamé cloth there might have been.

Had Walsh been writing a prescription for Jem? Bone was about to have this checked when Locker looked in. 'We've got Prestbury here, complaining.'

'We'll see him. Have you got someone checking whether Jem or anyone noticed a biro mark on Walsh's right hand?'

'That's being done, sir.'

Bone put his suit jacket on, covered up all the investigative material on the desk, and nodded.

Prestbury's dark little eyes, lurking under pale lids, fixed on Bone as he was brought in. He said,

'You kept me waiting, young man,' and rested his knuckles on the desk in an assertive manner. Bone glanced, and said, 'You've done a very, very silly thing.'

Prestbury stared. 'My good man, your manner leaves a lot to be desired. I'd have you remember whom you're speaking to. Precisely what are you talking about?'

'I'm talking about a gold monstrance and a thousand pounds and a man with a criminal record.'

Prestbury looked for the chair he had ignored, and sat down. He chewed the inside of his under-lip, cogitating. Bone said nothing, leaning back in his chair, turning down the bent corner of a folder as he met Prestbury's darting glance with judicial calm. He gave Prestbury a silent brownie point for not saying 'I don't know what you're talking about', but he wondered what the man would say when the silence became too much for him. He sat there, a grey, solid, smallish figure in a grey tweed suit, the short-cut grey hair, grey eyebrows beginning to attain the wildness of age. Bone felt 'The Grey Brother' would have been more appropriate.

'I cannot expect you to understand the religious aspect,' he said at last, 'that I was willing to pay a good deal of money to assure that a vessel once blessed by the presence of Our Lord should be placed and kept in a sanctified place and properly venerated.'

'From what little I know of the Catholic church, I don't believe it condones inciting a criminal act, or receiving stolen goods. You certainly did the former, and seem to have contemplated the latter without any sense of your position.'

'It's a case of the lesser evil and the greater good.'

'You are of course at liberty to jeopardize your own position, but what about tempting a man to commit a crime?'

'The man in question was perfectly willing.'

'I'm glad that you're satisfied. I wonder, really, how a confessor would see it.'

A faint mottling of Prestbury's cheeks betrayed how pale, until now, he had been, and less self-composed than Bone had thought. He went on, 'That's none of my business, I agree. To me, however, your action doesn't chime in with any-thing I've learnt about religion. It still seems to me, from the secular point of view, a very, very silly thing to have done.'

'You're charging me, are you?'

'As a magistrate, Mr Prestbury, can you tell me what option there is in the matter?'

Prestbury chewed his lip again for an appreciable minute. Finally he said, 'No.'

Bone let him think about that before he con-tinued. 'As this is a murder enquiry, we could ask for a warrant to search your house.'

'Search my house? What connection has my house, or I, to do with the murder?'

'We should like to examine any typewriters you may have.'

Prestbury sat up straighter, leant back, and folded his arms.

'I don't know what you mean,' he said.

Now what would have served you better, Bone thought, would have been to say *Typewriters! What have typewriters to do with it?* 'We'd like to compare their products with some letters that have been received threatening someone wth death and damnation. Though I thought that damnation was the province of St Peter.'

'I don't think it's a joking matter.'

'No, nor do I. So you have no objection to our looking at your typewriter?'

Prestbury said, 'I have the strongest objection to your doing anything of the sort.'

'Why?'

There was silence. Finally Bone charged him, only with conspiracy to steal, leaving the uttering of threats; for the present.

That dealt with, Bone felt one area had been cleared. He was left with Walsh's possession of the monstrance, Somerton's disappearance and the blackmail lists which might give yet more possibilities. He should see Jay Tansley-Ferrars, to check that 'J' and the photograph of the colour-bearer. He looked at the photocopies of the lists of money from Hervey's book. The dates were interesting: Hervey seemed to have applied to victims in rotation, never too often to any one person, no vast amounts at one time. He had it worked out on a business basis. For some reason, this seemed more dislikeable than if he had been rapacious.

Blane had found only the J that corresponded to anyone on the guest list. Bone turned the page and came on the drawing of entwined snakes. It struck him that snakes twined were the sign of Mercury, of medicine. Was it Walsh? No connection between Hervey and Walsh had yet shown up, and there wasn't the stick, what was the name of it, the caduceus. But then it might be any doctor at all, someone in Chelsea, or a doctor with a place in the country that Hervey might have seen. Did Walsh live in a house of importance? He was the only doctor at Cryer's on the night of the death. Bone scanned the list. There was Sutton Somerton, last seen by Edwina Marsh . . .

'You bleeding idiot,' Bone said to himself. Double snakes, SS, a tall man as Mary Highmountain had said, a better runner than Walsh except for the monstrance. Bone went out to find Blane, sifting through the stack of letters, papers, manuscripts and loose-leaf folders from Hervey's flat.

'We're looking for something to do with Somerton,' he said, putting the snake-adorned page before Blane. 'This may be relevant.'

Blane blew out his lips. 'Can't think why I didn't see it, sir.'

'Keep a healthy scepticism, Jack. It may not be Somerton. I just think it probably is.'

He phoned Prue Grant's house to check on Charlotte. Mrs Grant said she'd asked her to stay the night. The girls were watching television. Did he want to talk to Cha?

'No. I know she's all right with you. Thank you for asking her to stay.'

'I know you don't like her to be alone when Mrs Ames isn't there.'

'Thank you. I don't.'

'They're going round to feed the cat, and they'll come back here. I'll send them to bed early as they're sure to talk half the night.'

'Holiday time,' said Bone indulgently.

'Wretched children,' she agreed.

No word yet of Somerton, who seemed to have evaporated, black Volvo and all. Walsh still unconscious.

Bone and Locker dined at the Swan, were flirted with by June, the chief waitress, and then set off in the beginnings of dusk for Biddenden. Jay might be the key to the whole blackmail affair. Locker followed in his own car, because he was going to fetch Cherry from her parents' house at Hawkhurst on the way back. The sunlight had left the fields, and touched only some high trees on a hill past Sissinghurst Castle, and then it made a magnificence out of the clouds, and in Bone's driving mirror he could see the western sky flame and triumph. Warm air, cooled only a little by Bone's moderate speed, came in at the open windows. He thought of Grizel.

He remembered the boy in *The Snow Queen*, with the splinter of mirror in his heart that turned it to ice and dulled all feeling. Perhaps his own ice was starting to thaw. Would Grizel be going away for the holidays? She had spoken of the kitten getting used to her house during the holidays, as if she expected to be there. Teachers usually rushed abroad, or to the sea, to forget the children at as great a distance as possible. He had a sudden

174

picture of her, drinking in one of those little beach restaurants in Greece, smiling at him over the tumbler, her face shadowed by the vines overhead, but her eyes in a shaft of sunlight, glass-clear, the picture so vivid, so instant that he wondered, as it could not come from the past, if it belonged to his future.

A van, crowding behind him on the narrow road, hooted and flashed headlights. Bone got over to the side and concentrated on his driving.

Although it was scarcely dusk, the lights from the timbered pub shone out. People sat on a bench overlooking the handsome stones of the pavement, but a glimpse of the bar made Bone wish, not for the cosiness of a bar but for that of home, of turning his reading lamp on in the summer twilight, putting up his feet, taking a book and a drink, talking to Cha. She'd be having her supper with Grue. Lucky all those who could be at home.

Here was Jay's home, and lights shone cheerfully in the windows there. As Bone pushed open the gate, which swung unlatched, he heard a high keening sound and thought of the disappearing dog. The note was sustained at an almost unbearable pitch, stopped with a muffled sob that was nearly human and, having thus caught breath, started the same keen again. Bone, going down the path, saw the front door was ajar and felt, all at once, cold.

He stopped just inside it, Locker nearly bumping into him. He called, 'Is anyone there?' That poem about the traveller, with ghosts listening, crowding the stair. Somewhere the dog stopped, took breath, began again. The place felt wrong, smelt wrong. He looked in at the war-games room, saw nothing but the ranks of soldiers waiting for the next manoeuvre in the half-light. He turned to the room where he had talked to Jay. The wailing intensified as he pushed open the door.

The scene was one familiar to him from break-ins: furniture, pictures, brutally displaced, a confusion of fury. The sofa was thrust askew, the wall cupboard where the soldiers stood that Shay had admired, gaped wounded with broken glass.

Bone, the back of his neck acrawl, took a careful step inside until he could see the sofa. The dog sat there, oblivious in his wailing, catching his breath, then flinging up his small head in a long sound of misery. A man lay crumpled on the carpet, in sleeveless teeshirt and jeans, one arm under him, the head towards Bone and bent aside. The carpet, the front of the sofa, were horribly gaudy with the blood whose smell was now so strong. There was almost no side to the head. The shoulder and arm were shattered by manic blows.

Locker at his back drew breath, as he had done, in shock.

'That Mr Tansley-Ferrars, sir?'

It wasn't. The body was too well-built, the hair that still showed was blond.

'It's likely to be the friend he lives with, Magnus someone. Can't see the dog doing that for a guest.'

The dog had stopped at their voices, and now

whimpered, putting his nose to the man's head and looking up at Bone, at Locker, appealing to have this happening explained, reversed.

'I'll go and call in, sir.'

'Right.'

Bone clicked his fingers to the dog, which after a moment came round the sofa, hesitant, trembling, its tail clamped down. Bone said, 'Come on, fella. You don't want to be in here.' Needing reassurance, company, the dog crept nearer, still whining, until Bone could pick him up and go out. He listened for any sound in the house. A tap dripped. There was silence.

The ring of trees at the back of the house had lost the evening light and stood dark and mysterious as a sorcerer's wood. The dog in Bone's arms juddered with intermittent trembling, and every now and then moaned. Caring for animals after their owners' violent death seemed to be Bone's present role in the world. He stood in the front garden by the door. There was no sign of a break-in here.

He could see blood on the dog's muzzle. It might have tried to rouse Magnus. Two women passed, and looked at Bone with the glum disapproval of seeing what is out of the ordinary and unaccountable, a man by an open door, with a shivering dog, watching the street. A woman came out of the next house, locked her door and walked to her car.

'Glad you've stopped him howling,' she said. 'It was giving me the creeps.'

'What time did he start?' Bone asked.

'Oh, ages ago.' She was about to sit in behind

the wheel when he said sharply, 'An hour? Two hours?' and she halted.

'Well . . . I heard him when I turned off the play on the box. That'd be ten.'

'Did you hear anything else?'

'No. These houses are very solid, you know, we don't hear neighbours much; and they're detached. It's not like living in a terrace. Is anything wrong?'

'An unhappy dog,' Bone said. She shrugged, got into the car, her car, backed it out, and was gone. How lucky for you, he thought, that you didn't come round an hour ago to see what the matter might be. You wouldn't have liked it.

Locker's car slid to a stop behind his.

'On their way,' he said as he came up the path.

'I'd like to know where Tansley-Ferrars is.'

'Think it's him, sir? A domestic, as you might say?'

'It's not a break-in. I'd like to know.'

They waited. It was a long wait.

A car glided to a stop, head-on to Bone's, the man inside ducked to look at them and then swiftly got out. He came along the pavement running. 'It's Tansley-Ferrars,' Bone murmured.

'Doesn't look like a domestic then. Hardly come back, would he?' As Jay came running, Bone thought that criminal deviousness could result in almost any unexpected behaviour. The sort of ménage here . . . he thought of Orton and Halliwell. What he could not imagine was Jay killing Magnus with the dog there; or leaving the dog to find him.

The dog convulsed under his arm, trying even

to wag its tail. Jay, pale and frightened, reached for it.

'Something's wrong. What is it? I knew something was wrong. Right back up the road . . .' He caught the dog's distress as he took it in his arms, and gazed at Bone. He too looked for reassurance, for Authority to say that all was well.

'I'm sorry. Something is very wrong. I believe it is your friend—'

Jay moved to go in, Bone blocked him and he straight-armed Bone in the chest with startling force sending him back onto Locker. When they caught up, he had found the room with the light on and was standing at the end of the sofa, the shuddering dog trying to escape, held obliviously hard. Jay was completely still, then he gasped, and went on drawing breath through his mouth as if all the air in the room was too thin to sustain him.

'Come out, please.' Bone drew him back, and he came as far as the door and stood there.

'I knew there was something. I knew this morning it was a bad day.' He spoke in a desperate whisper, in spasms. 'When I said goodbye, I thought, I shan't see you again. But I'd thought that before. You get these feelings. You tell yourself it's all cobblers. Why didn't I *believe* it?'

The dog moaned and licked his face. He looked, suddenly, middle-aged, the lines of grief on his forehead and in crows' feet, and twisting his mouth.

A noise of arrival outside fetched Locker away.

'Come out, please. Nothing must be touched.'

Jay came. Once out of the house he took Bone by surprise, turning to hurry round the house to the terrace, and stood looking in at the room. The fizzing lightning of photoflash silhouetted him and made the dog bark.

'You had better sit in one of the cars.'

'I won't go. I won't leave here. I should have stayed with him. God, why am I so squeamish? I couldn't touch him and I owe him that. Oh God. How shall I live? Who could—who *could*? Who could do that? We don't know people like that.' Bone, however, thought sourly: Almost anyone, you find, given the right, or the wrong, circumstances. He pivoted one of the white iron chairs round, and put Jay into it. He sat, resistless, watching the flash that bleached him and made the trees jump into sight beyond him.

Bone said, 'If you're sure you want to be here.'

Locker, in protective slippers and an overall, had moved in after the camera. Bone rapped on the glass, Locker saw him and pointed them out to the team. The police surgeon came in, crouched, spoke and moved about with his back to the window.

'I ought to be in there with him.'

'I'm sorry.'

Jay put the dog down on his knees, but it scrambled up again to lie against his chest, and he held it so.

'Is this part of what happened to Alex?'

'We don't know yet.'

'Magnus wasn't there at Ken's. He wasn't well. He shouldn't have got up today at all.'

Light overhead, from a small window eyebrowed in thatch, shone on the leaves. Jay glanced up.

180

'That's his room. Oh, damn, damn. They have to. Of course.'

'Yes.'

At length they moved Magnus, blocking the view with solid backs as they moved him onto the stretcher. Locker appeared at the corner of the house with a torch, and Bone crossed to him.

'Would Mr Tansley-Ferrars be able to make identification now, do you think? We've arranged things. It's all right to look at.'

Bone went back to ask Jay, who got up with an effort. They went round the house in the warm night air. The hall carpet was covered in plastic. The stretcher stood in the wider part of the hall by the kitchen at the foot of the stairs, and blankets had been arranged to cover the plastic wrapping and everything but the face.

Jay said, 'It's Magnus. Magnus Haywood.' Bone caught the flat note of final acceptance. There would have been the wild irrational hope that it somehow wasn't.

'Where do you take him?'

Bone did not at once answer, and the dark eyes glanced in question. Jay pushed a tear aside with the ball of his thumb and said, 'Oh yes. Hell. Oh shit. *The morgue*, isn't it. Look, could I be with him a minute? I won't touch if I'm not supposed to. Just a minute to say goodbye.'

Bone withdrew to the corner. Locker went silently back to the scene of crime. Bone could see out of the front door. There were people standing across the road talking and staring, a little crowd. A cigarette glowed and faded by the ambulance.

Cars passed, slowing as they saw the ambulance, the police cars, the little crowd. Music came from windows open on the night air, a pop tune from a car, a piano concerto and the soundtrack of a TV film from houses. Bone found he was standing cramped as if against cold.

Jay had not moved, until now when he came to join Bone and said 'Thank you,' politely. Bone sent the PC for the ambulance men.

He took Tansley-Ferrars into the war room, where the new-vacuumed carpet and the grey dust here and there showed the team's traces. Jay put the dog down, and it went about the room sniffing.

'You'd been away all day.'

'I went to Bedlam. I mean the Imperial War Museum. A lecture there this afternoon. Part of a series. I suppose you have to be sure I didn't kill him. Well, I was . . .' He had gone to the window and watched the stretcher taken out. He went on in an iron, constrained tone. 'I was there from one thirty until six. I stayed to talk to Chilham, and he gave me tea. Then I called on my brother. He's not a reliable witness, but his landlady is. I paid the rent. Then I came home, and apart from the usual snarl-up at the end of the bypass it didn't take that long. I don't know what time I left Leo's.' He had lit a cigarette.

'His address.'

'Forty-three, Whippett's Avenue, Kensington. It's off Marloes Road, but you'll want the phone number, won't you?' He gave it. Bone wrote it, but it would not be a telephone check. One of

Blane's people would go there, taking time from Blane's check of Cryer's guests in London.

Jay slumped suddenly into a chair, a worn leather one with padded back and carving round the edge. He moved his head only slightly when Locker came in and mutely asked Bone if he could speak to Jay.

'Mr Tansley-Ferrars, was a message for you on the kitchen memo pad this morning?'

'No. Well, I mean there had been. Magnus . . .' he stumbled on it and drew breath. 'He wiped it when we were clearing breakfast.'

'There's a message, sir: *J ring V.*'

'He always wrote things down. Memory like a sieve so he always wrote things down. V? Who the hell's V? I don't know any V. You see he'd expect to tell me,' he said desolately. 'I can't think. My coat's in the car with my address book, so I'd better—'

Locker spoke to someone in the hall, who could be heard going out to the car.

'I'm sorry,' Jay said. His face was white and shadows, cut out of paper. Bone said, aside to Locker, 'What about Cherry? Is she getting home all right?'

'Her dad's running her home. He doesn't like night driving but that's how it is.'

'Sorry.'

Locker gave a tight grin and shrugged.

'Verena,' Jay said. 'Verena Somerton? I wonder why I was supposed to ring her. I can't think of any other V.'

'In Tenterden, is that?' Locker asked.

'Yes, I'll ring her tomorrow,' Jay said as Locker went out. 'Have to see what she wants. I go there and chat, you know. She's one of those rather sad invalids.'

'Who is there you could stay with tonight?'

Jay raised his eyes. After a moment he took in what Bone was saying. 'Yes. Of course. Can't stay here. I don't suppose I'll live here any more.'

'There is something else I have to ask you about . . . It's Alex Hervey. He kept a photograph of a model soldier on a horse, carrying regimental colours. Can you tell me more about that?'

'Oh God. I suppose it's important. I stole it. I nicked it from Abel Fitzgalton's collection when he died. Alex had seen it there, Fitzi told him it was one of his favourites. He used to cadge the odd cash off me, pretending he'd give me away. I didn't mind. He was always good company, man or woman.'

'Did you know of anyone else he got money from, for other reasons?'

'No, did he?' Jay was not interested. His voice was lifeless. A PC knocked on the door and handed in Jay's jacket, a Welsh tapestry in grey and green. Bone gestured to him to leave it over a chair. As he went out, Locker returned, and stood holding the door open and looking at Bone, who went to him.

'Mrs Somerton hadn't asked them to ring her. She hadn't rung here at all. When I rang her, she thought we'd found her husband.'

'Step up that general call on him. Make it priority.'

If Verena Somerton hadn't asked Jay to phone her, then perhaps Sutton Somerton had. Perhaps Somerton had been here. There were prints on the heavy glass ashtray that had been the weapon, and they seemed almost too easy a clincher. How soon could identification come? Not soon enough for Bone, impatient to be away.

Whoever had come, it had not been a stranger, an intruder. The house had not been broken into, there were glasses and a bottle new opened and nearly empty. He had sat in the armchair. He had spatulate fingers, unlike the ovals of Jay and Magnus, visible everywhere in little aureoles of grey dust. He must have been here for some time. What in the world had suddenly blown in his brain, what could Magnus have said, have done? Was Sutton the murderer of Hervey?

Jay was telephoning to a friend, arranging to come for the night. Colonel Chilham, the Kensington landlady and his brother Leo all corroborated his account of himself.

Sergeant Shay came from the radio car and brought news. A black Volvo had been seen down the road earlier. The house-to-house had just brought in two sightings of it. Two ladies had disliked it being outside their house, partly blocking their entrance; they did not know it was a Volvo but described it well enough, 'And a kid across the road, ten-year-old, had seen it there. None of them caught sight of the driver, except one of the ladies, who thought he was tall.'

Black Volvos were not blue roses, but an unfamiliar one parked nearby at the right time – or the wrong if you saw it the fateful way – was significant. Bone said, 'I'll be at Saxhurst,' and looked in on Jay again. He was sitting in the leather chair, looking at nothing, stroking the dog.

The sight of Magnus' body had shaken Bone. He had seen horrific motorway pile-ups that evoked memory of his own car smash, but deliberate and vicious murder was another thing. He hoped he never would become inured to the sight. He wanted now to say to Jay *It will get worse for a time, then very slowly it gets bearable.* He said, 'I'm sorry,' and Jay raised his head and sighed.

'You've been kind.'

'We try. You'll let the sergeant know where you can be contacted.'

'Yes.'

Bone left him holding the dog to his face.

Soon after two in the morning, Littlestone police came through. The Volvo, parked askew on the grass before a house on the New Romney road, had blood on the steering wheel and the driver's door.

Bone, roused from a doze, said, 'Tell them we'll be down there. Are they getting up a search?'

'Getting it set, sir.'

Bone washed, hot water for comfort, cold afterwards to wake. The lights in the incident room were too bright. Someone had made coffee. It was disgusting but he drank it for the caffeine. One of the team was trying to shave at his desk. Bone, who had not had time, said nastily, 'We're leaving,' and he grabbed his jacket and came. They went out into the dark.

CHAPTER ELEVEN

They set off, low-voiced in the car park, Bone and Locker silent. Out on the road, Locker slept. Bone watched the road come towards them out of the dark, hedges and trees, sleeping houses, hollows the road swooped into and out of; pale villages, then again hedges and trees, with the life of the night showing sometimes in the glint of eyes. The sky in the north-east began to draw from the dark of earth, where dawn would come. The street of Appledore gave back their engine's sound, and the driver took the sharp corner over the old canal. Half-way across Romney Marsh they roused a heron that rose in magnificent flurry from the ditch, legs trailing in the gloom of the headlights as he bent into the night. The road snaked into Romney; New Romney; straightened out and came to Littlestone. Jam-sandwich police cars lined the road, a blue, brilliant light revolved. Bone got out into relative silence in which he could hear the wash and thud of the sea.

There were brief introductions. 'Your man, if it's him, may be on the beach still. A tall dark man was seen by a courting couple walk into the sea and wash himself. In his clothes.'

The strange image flowered in Bone's mind. They walked towards the sea, first tarmac and then a high kerb. Grey-green grasses rooted in sand sprang to life under a low-held torch. Beach huts loomed. Bone heard the local men had started at the far end and were working this way from the east. The tide, judging by the thunder and long, singing wash, was going out. They stood, in the small wind coming off the sea. The activity, the deployment of men, had brought people to their windows; heads showed against rectangles of light on the seafront buildings.

Here the beach was shallow, a silted harbour once leading to Romney. He could see the lights of Folkestone one way, Dungeness the other, arms of the bay, and to the south a haze of reddish pallor that might be Boulogne. The local inspector talked to Locker in a low voice. He could have done without Bone's presence.

Bone moved a short way onto the shingle, looking down to the sea and imagined a man walking into it and washing his clothes. *The moving waters at their priestlike task of pure ablution round earth's human shores . . .*

He looked up. The whole black depth of the sky with its uninterested stars hung over his head. Dizzy, he brought himself down and heard distant commotion along to the east. Inspector Hardiman started towards it. Torches and agitation seemed to be down by the sea, and Bone, his night eyes adjusted, went down the dry shingle that gave to his steps, over the damp compacted stones, onto the sand, and strode along there below the dark line of the tidewrack. To his left, Locker came parallel, big against the paling sky;

to his right, the melancholy, long, withdrawing roar.

He reached a breakwater, saw just in time that there was a pool alongside it, and walked up the stony sand to where he could step over. He put a hand on a half-seen damp post and one foot on the concrete sill, the other up to the wood, and stepped. He heard a guttural sound of alarm and a shape rose before him. He dropped on top of it. If it was an innocent sleeper, bad luck—

He felt the hard clout to his brow and chopped at the arm. Locker came avalanching down the ringing stones. Bone fell, caught hold of a cold ankle and hauled on it. Locker, grappling, bellowed. There were whistles and bobbing torches along the shore.

The man was swearing, a diarrhoea of dismal words in a contemptuous upper-class voice, and he kicked at Bone with the free foot until Locker dropped on his chest. The torches arrived, hands pulled the three men to their feet. Locker identified Somerton, hanging pallid between two uniformed men, his mouth a hard, thin line, his eyes glaring. They took him away up the beach.

'Are you all right, sir?' Locker demanded, peering at Bone in the torchlight. His tone and look made Bone aware that he wasn't, that his head hurt and, now that he was standing, a sluggish warm substance was making its way down his forehead towards his eye. Hardiman arrived, and exclaimed.

'Sorry,' Bone said. 'I'd no business to be here.' He held a tissue to what seemed an extraordinarily

189

tender place on the hairline. 'Should have stayed where I was put.'

'We caught a tramp over there and thought it was your man. He was abusive enough.'

'So was ours,' said Bone. He was beginning to feel unsure of his legs, and reached for Locker. They gave him a hand up the sliding shingle. Hardiman sent a PC for Bone's car.

'We'll get you to the station, sir, and get the doctor. Very satisfying for you to have got Somerton yourselves.'

Bone said that the formal arrest must still, of course, be made by Hardiman and credited to his force. He congratulated him on the operation. Hardiman audibly warmed. Ahead of them as they crossed the grass there was another skirmish as Somerton made a violent effort to free himself. The convulsion of figures in the half-light and torchlight turned Bone's stomach and he said, 'Sorry. Let me be a moment,' pushed aside from his supporters and threw up. Swivelling torchlight identified what he was doing and compassionately shifted. Locker was there, diffident but alarmed.

'There's a bench here,' someone called.

'That's right, sir. Sit down over here till the car comes.' They sat him down, and he leant forward. Something dark splashed on the stones by his feet, and again. Locker held a handkerchief to Bone's head and the splashes stopped. Someone came with a first aid tin. With a dressing on his head, and feeling a perfect fool, Bone got into his car. He was developing the Mother of Headaches.

The police surgeon accommodated him with a

few stitches and a dressing, shone a light into each eye and told him to avoid energetic activity for twenty-four hours and to see his doctor in the morning.

'You mean later today?' Bone said.

'I'd recommend a couple of days' sick-leave myself.'

'It's all right. We can hope the shouting's over for the present.'

'Considering the man had a stone in his fist, you got off very lightly. It was a glancing blow and there's a small degree of concussion. Don't mess with it. Here's a couple of tablets. One now, you get home to your bed and take the other, and don't go springing about within the next twenty-four hours.'

Bone wished his bed were next door and not an hour's drive away, but the tablet worked before they were half across the Marsh, distancing him from the headache. It was early light. He remembered the heron but it was not to be seen.

Locker kept glancing at him with concern. He said, 'I'm all right, Steve. You'll be able to mop up without me in your hair. Make a change.'

'Don't worry about it, sir.'

'I'm not worrying. It's what the doctor handed out. Very sedative. Makes it hard to give a tinker's about anything. But later on I shall be howling with curiosity.'

'We'll keep you in the picture.'

They drove up a long hill into sunlight. It was behind them all the way to Saxhurst, where Steve got out. Bone drowsed on the road to Tunbridge

Wells. The driver came up to the flat with him, saying he had his orders, and saw Bone into bed; and he was reduced enough to be glad of it.

He lay looking at the sunlight behind the curtains, and thought that at breakfast time he would ring the Grants' house to warn Cha of a damaged father before she came home. He thought of Magnus Haywood, battered to death by the same hand that had felled him with a stone. Cha could have lost her other parent.

The cat Ziggy stopped washing, and settled on his feet.

He woke because someone in the room had exclaimed, and he rolled over and remembered, by lying on it, the wound to his head. Charlotte, rigid in the doorway, was holding Ziggy in her arms and he was struggling because her grip was so tight.

'Hallo, pet. Sorry, just a whack on the head. What time is it? I meant to ring you.'

'Ih'thenn,' Charlotte said, and with an effort repeated, 'It's ten.'

'Damned pills he gave me. I'm all right, though, just woozy from sedative. Zig's had no breakfast, by the way, he's not lying for once. Can I have some fruit juice, pet?'

'M'm. Course.' She waved, a flitter of the fingers, and went downstairs. He called after her, 'Don't worry. It really is nothing. I'll get up soon.'

'Okay.'

She reappeared with a tumbler of grapefruit juice, and Ziggy's fervid attendance showed she hadn't waited to feed him.

'Bless you.' He sat up gingerly, and drank.

'Are you really truly all right? Not just stiff upper lip?'

He looked up at her. She had her hair in plaits tied together on her chest with string. Her teeshirt said Archangel is Heaven. Her jeans had a tear on the left knee.

'Yes, darling, I am all right. Very sorry you had the shock. This – does it look very bad?' She nodded – 'It's just a bad graze and a cut. The stitches probably look worst. I meant to ring you, but the wretched pills made me sleep on.'

Ziggy put his head down on Charlotte's foot and walked, stropping his teeth on her toes. She was in flipflops and one of her scars showed along the instep, silvery, between an avenue of stitch marks. He said, 'We're a tough lot. Tough as old Bones. Come on, feed that fur stomach down there. What do you mean to do today?'

'Look after you,' she said, and, leaning over, switched his phone extension off. At the door she stopped. 'Have you got concussion?'

'Slightly. Nothing serious.'

'Then you don't get up.'

'I'm fine, Cha.'

'You don't get up,' she said, shooting out a finger. 'If you do, I phone Auntie Alison.'

Bone lay back. 'Don't shoot, Colonel. I surrender.'

'I sh' think so.' She went downstairs hampered by Ziggy, and he heard her moving about in the kitchen. The phone in the sitting-room rang and she answered it. She rang off and he called out to know who it was.

'Steve. I told him what you told me, that you are all right. He says he will come later.'

Bone noticed that she was not speaking well. The blurred Oriental l-sounds were a regression. He wished he had set the alarm to wake in time to warn her.

It'll sure cure me of walking stupidly into maniacs, he thought. Shortly he would phone Steve.

He slept.

The sunlight had moved. He sat up with reasonable care, and realized that what had woken him was the door bell, for he heard Charlotte talking on the entryphone. She opened the door. Feet came swift and light on the lower stairs. Grue Grant, he supposed. The voices, though, had not the tones of Cha and Grue talking. They were quiet and slightly formal. Then he caught the second voice's Scots, and hoped to Heaven that Cha did not let Grizel into a stuffy room, to an unshaven wreck.

But Grizel's voice gently overbore Charlotte's. The light feet came higher. He saw her in the doorway and said, 'On your peril come in.'

'My peril. I've already been told that Daddy would hate it, and I've ignored that. You speak far too clearly for bad concussion. Your motor centres are in better nick than Charlotte's this morning.'

'You are horrid, Mrs Shaw,' Cha said, arriving. They came in together, Grizel with her hand on Charlotte's shoulder, both smiling.

'Open a window, Cha – but not the curtains,' he said.

Grizel moved a chair to sit near the bed.

'She came to see how *I* was,' Cha säid from behind the curtains, which as she manoeuvred let in enough light to make Bone shade his eyes. He saw anxiety in Grizel's face, and wondered how alarming he looked. He could not be looking as alarming as when Locker had been alarmed, but then Locker, by reason of his profession, had a high alarm-level.

'Yes, I thought it was Cha who was likely to be still a wee bit invalidish; I didn't look for it to be you. How is your head, and what happened to it?'

'Someone resisting arrest happened to it. But I'm fine.'

'If that's fine, I shall have to revize my opinions of the phrase entirely. You resemble – let me think – Banquo's ghost, let's say after a stay at a health farm. Improved but not wholly alive.'

He found that laughing hurt him, and lay back.

'Has the doctor seen you today?'

'No.'

'He should. And of course you'll not get up until he says.'

She had a khaki shirt and trousers today, crisp enough for a safari in the darkest heart of Tunbridge Wells. The shirt, by inadvertence or carefree intent, was open far enough to show the slight hollow of cleavage. This was unfair, and he kept his eyes on her face – mostly. Charlotte said hospitably, 'I'll make some tea. Or d'you like coffee, Mrs Shaw?'

'Tea would be nice.'

Charlotte was off downstairs. Ziggy arrived,

however. He was taking advantage fully of there being someone in bed, and he jumped up and made bread on the counterpane for a little.

'The little cat I'm to have is darker than this one. I tried Charlotte's advice and the one who liked me was a tabby with a white patch beside his nose. Emily said I should name him when I've observed him a while. Why was this one called Ziggy?'

'I've reason to believe his full name is Ziggy Stardust.'

'After that doomed seventies rock-star? I've heard of a corgi called Oliver Twist because he was always hungry; but he was a dog. The naming of cats is far more serious.'

He lay there, content with her presence, as she went on talking about Emily and the cats. Charlotte brought tea and biscuits, and sat on the floor with her cup, by the bed, now and then stroking Ziggy. He could see she was happy with two people she liked, and wondered if it would trouble her when she realized they were interested in each other – for he was acutely aware that Grizel was interested in him. In this light her eyes were very green.

He was annoyed when the bell rang again. Charlotte went to answer, opened the downstairs door and called up 'It's Steve.'

'I'll be off,' Grizel said. 'I hope he knows not to stay long.' She finished her tea, and her eyes smiled above the cup. 'I shall come again, to be sure you are not taking risks.'

Locker arrived, and she stood up to go. Bone knew from Locker's attentive bemused regard that he too found Mrs Shaw an attractive woman. Charlotte appeared with another teacup and cried, 'Oh, you're not going!'

'I must. Your father has fifteen minutes of work to be done. Inspector Locker's brought a file with him.'

'Fifteen minutes,' said Charlotte bodefully. She gave Locker a cup of rather brewed tea, knowing he quite liked it. Though they shut the door, Bone could hear them talking away downstairs. He would have asked her to stay to lunch, almost had done so, when it came to him that there might not be anything in the house for a guest. With Mrs Ames away, their catering was extempore.

Locker sat on the bedfoot. He was wary of small chairs, having broken one at the station, an event now part of their folklore. The chair stayed there facing the bed, reminding Bone.

'So how's the shop?'

'Somerton won't speak. One solitary utterance was "Tell my wife I'm sorry about the letters" and when I asked him what letters, he said, "*She* knows. She has them," and that was it. The man just shut his mouth. But she hasn't had any letters that it could be. I went over there of course, and she was up out of bed on walking-sticks. I asked could she manage and she said, "I must". She has no idea what letters he could mean. She calls him Cecil.'

'Cecil. *Cecil?* Those letters . . . I saw the name on some of Hervey's letters, that Blane has. That's it. He's Cecil to his women. I can't think why. It's a name I'd pay not to have. It must be a middle name.'

'First name, sir. It's his first name. Mrs Somerton

says he never uses it professionally. But there you are, he used it to Alix Hamilton. And they were what I can only call hot stuff. I'd skimmed through, I was going through a pile of things, they were Blane's pidgin really. Pitiful. Crawling letters about how she mastered him, and putting the boot in; and some stuff as explicit as a biology book. And written of course to the woman he thought Hervey was. Calling himself her good dog, and how if he was not good she would correct him . . . Jack Blane and I aren't given to seeing eye to eye, but he said he needed a sick-bag handy when he was going through that little lot. Hervey must have been a real little turd.'

'And these would be the letters Somerton thought his wife had.'

'I reckon so. You know, I don't see how this Hervey could be that good an impersonator. I mean, these drag acts.'

'But you're thinking of drag acts where the whole point is that everyone knows it's a man: Danny La Rue, Edna Everage, Charley's Aunt. Here there's a man whose private joke it is that he can be a woman so well that people don't know. He must have worked on it, thrown himself into it, observed and copied and practised. I wouldn't have believed it either but Cryer and Serafin and Tansley-Ferrars all told me; and the appearance was totally convincing. Hervey could turn from a slightly too good-looking man into a very glamorous woman.'

'But wouldn't men know? Chemistry and that?'

'It seems they didn't. Of course we're detectives,

198

you couldn't pull the wool over our eyes, we can tell a wrong'un a mile away, can't we?'

'Life should be so easy,' Locker admitted.

'I've believed in acting, on the TV or screen; or even in the theatre where you're in an audience. You know it's not real, but you can still want to weep. Hervey took it a step further. We're forced to believe he could, and if the pheromones were wrong, the chemistry, it still seems to have convinced. I dare say he's not the only one. Think of those women who've gone to war, living among men as a man. In these hygienic days they couldn't do it, but in those days they didn't even undress the wounded unless they had a body wound. The world's a lot odder than it seems. There was a French man, I forget his name, nobody was sure which sex he was at all. The Chevalier something. It's amazing.'

'But this bondage stuff. Part of his liking to manipulate that Serafin talked of? But that goes past everything.'

'He must have wanted to deceive on a more spectacular scale. I imagine if you want to despise people in a big way, that's quite a reasonable set-up. They say professionals don't waste energy despising the punters, they merely go through the motions, but we have to remember Hervey was not a pro. He was in it for the fun.'

'What about Somerton?'

'That's for a psychiatrist; but I'd say that all hostility is resentment that has to have somewhere to go, and he made himself his target. He might feel punishment purged him, left him free to get angry again. I don't understand the sex side, why it has to be a woman to punish. Oedipal, I suppose, a fixation on power figures from childhood. If they thought it was a man with a whip it would spoil the relationship, the game. It would have been *kinky*.'

Locker snorted. 'Well, then. Say Hervey *told* Somerton he'd sent the letters to his wife. That'd be a power play in a big way, a real nasty one. He calculated Somerton's response wrong and maybe hadn't seen the gun in the drawer.'

'Too wrapped up in the game being played. We'll never know.'

Steve contemplated this a moment and then said, 'It's interesting. There's not always time to theorize. Oh, and Dr Walsh, he came round this morning. What happened was, he glanced into the bedroom and saw "the woman in the gold dress" trying the monstrance against her dress like a brooch or something, looking in the mirror over the chest there. He knew what the thing was because he'd been shown it by Ken Cryer, and he was angry. Not meant to adorn a body. Oddly enough he told the woman that vanity would find her out, which it looks as if it did. But she wouldn't put the thing down, she kept trying it against her bosom or her waist. Then she held it on top of her head and swung her hips about, and sort of smirked at him, and he saw he was dealing with a fool and he got it off her after a bit of a struggle, he shook her; and yes, he did have biro on his hand. He got the monstrance and shut it in his bag to give to Cryer and tell him to take better care of it. He left the woman giggling fit to split. He thought she was drunk or stoned on something. On his way down he was given a message about Mrs Wheatley; and Cryer had no time for him because Serafin was leaving, so he became impatient and left, along with Serafin, taking advantage, he says, of the gate being opened by the security guard for Serafin's car. He forgot the monstrance and was horrified, at Mrs Wheatley's, to find he'd still got it. But he decided to phone Cryer to tell him he had it, and to shut it in the drugs cabinet overnight and take it to him in the morning. He didn't figure on having it bust out of his hands by a drunken driver.'

'All very smooth and understandable.'

Charlotte opened the door and stood there.

'Ah, I think that's my fifteen minutes,' Locker said.

'Cha's watch is fast. I'm sure it's not as long.'

Charlotte said, 'If you promise not to talk shop, there is soup, and scrambled eggs, for lunch.'

'No, I must be going on. Thanks for the offer, Charlotte. Another day.'

Bone could tell, and hoped Locker could not, that Cha was relieved. Locker stood by the bed saying, 'Well, how soon do we see you?'

'Tomorrow, I should think.'

'Doctor has to see him first,' Cha said, truculent. 'He's concussed.'

'Only very mildly.'

'You look a lot better now,' Locker stated comfortably.

'He *what*? How did he look at first?'

'Spare my vanity. I need a shave. Earlier on I needed a new head. So I've improved and I'd rather hear no more about it.'

It was one of the longest days he had ever spent. Cha brought him his razor, and a hand mirror. The process left him feeling odd in the head and slightly nauseated. He lay down carefully. Intending to warn Cha to bring the razor first, then the guests, another time, he gave up because of the obvious snag that after the business of shaving he was in no state for guests.

He ate very little of the scrambled eggs, told Charlotte that one could survive without solids for days, and reminded her that Ziggy went a bundle on scrambled egg. Still, the bend of the head as she went out with his plate upset him. She called from the stairs, 'I phoned the doctor and you're to keep quiet. He'll come this evening.'

'What a competent young rabbit you are,' he said.

He dozed. Charlotte talked on the phone and watched television. The sunlight shifted from the windows. His mirror had shown him a surprising pallor and an extensive contusion from under the dressing. He dozed again, and then lay trying not to think. Cha brought him beef tea and dry toast, which was welcome. He complained of boredom. Cha brought her headphone cassette player and some of his tapes. This was better, although he fell asleep listening and ran the battery down. He woke with one of those full-fledged ideas: *I can never marry her. She can never become Grizel Bone*, and he was desolated.

The doctor arrived in the middle of this bitter thought, and shone lights into his eyes, gave him a new dressing, and repeated the ban on reading and television.

'What about getting to work?'

His doctor, an old acquaintance, snapped his bag shut and said, 'I wish I'd ten pounds for every fool who rushes back to work. Or if I were well paid when my patients were ill, I'd encourage it. Back to work, I'd say, and have them nicely on my hands again in no time. But your concussion is very slight, or you'd have been put in hospital for observation. You'll not hurt if you don't drive a car; get people to read things to you; avoid a VDU or a TV as much as you can. Act with normal sense. You've no double vision and you're doing nicely. Oh, and no violent movement, no jogging or unarmed combat. Stick to music for your entertainment, so long as you don't boogie to the beat. Get Charlotte to read to you. Does she still?'

'No. The therapist says she doesn't need that any longer. She's doing very little therapy now.'

'Amazing girl. I couldn't believe who it was on the telephone. Perhaps not clear as a bell but distinct, confident.'

'She's worried. It makes her speech thicker.'

'I shall perform an act of charity: I shall reassure her. Good-day to you, Robert. Come to evening surgery tomorrow, please.'

Bone fitted the ear-pieces in place and went back to Mozart, clear as new batteries and Murray Perahia could make him.

CHAPTER TWELVE

At the station, Bone had to smile away references to his head. It looked alarming, he had to admit, and it felt swollen. He was tender of it, avoiding contact, he noticed, even with blowing curtains.

Locker brought Somerton to his room. He lined up the folder on the desk before him, aware both of faint headache and of excitement. This really, after all, appeared to be the villain. He repressed the sense of guilt at not having got on to Somerton before Magnus Haywood's death, and was grateful a third victim hadn't been himself. When he was still a sergeant, his Inspector had told him: everyone makes mistakes, luckily even villains.

Unconsciously cupping a careful hand over his injury, he looked again at the letters written by Cecil Sutton Somerton to Alix Hamilton. He noted the spiky, agitated handwriting with huge loops in the upper cases, which according to graphologists meant fantasy. There was fantasy enough in these letters, so complicated a fantasy that it was definitely pornography. In paperback they might make a fortune – *The Beat Generation?*

The fantasist had been escorted by two heavy-shouldered PCs, both shorter than he was, however. Bone was startled at his height. Somehow, his memory of the shadowy figure that had

204

loomed over him on the beach had the quality of nightmare, but Somerton really was as tall as that. He could give Mick Parsons several inches.

Somerton sat, staring at Bone with round, gloomy eyes. He had a curiously affronted air, lent perhaps by the close-shut mouth, while the high forehead made him seem intellectual. The long neck set on sloping shoulders lent a weakness, a giraffe without that grace and distinction. His dark suit was rumpled, but he shot rather grubby cuffs with a fussy care as he settled himself.

'I hear, Mr Somerton, that you've not been able to help with our enquiries.'

Somerton maintained his offended glare. Bone waited, then moved the papers, glancing down. Somerton glanced too. His long arm pointed across the desk, and one of the PCs came sharply to his side.

'My wife gave you those. They are private letters!'

Strange that a murderer should conceive any part of his life to be still private. His invasion of other lives had been ruthless enough. But he had spoken.

'Your wife didn't have them,' Bone said.

Silence. A twitch. Amazed eyes.

'They were found in Alex Hervey's flat. The flat he used as Alix Hamilton.'

'Impossible.' The hazel-green eyes were certain of the truth, therefore Bone was lying. 'She told me she had sent them to my wife. To Verena. I was prepared to pay. It would have killed her. Your men took the money away.'

'They gave you a receipt, I believe.' Bone supposed 'her' to be Somerton's wife. Certainly the letters had killed Alex Hervey. He observed that Somerton referred to Alex as 'she' as though he had not taken in Bone's statement about his identity.

'These letters. You were going to pay for them, you say. You were being blackmailed.'

'Of course.' Impatient, a schoolmaster with a slow pupil, Somerton flicked a hand. 'It was all a deception. A vicious joke among them all. They were all in it.'

To Bone's dismay he began crying, with little noisy undignified gulps, a giraffe with indigestion. He thought of Lamia Hervey's tears when she thought she had killed the man she loved. She had thought Alix Hamilton was laughing at her; so, it seemed, had Somerton. Then there were Tansley-Ferrars' few tears, cried for the man he shared his life with, and no doubt for himself and his desolation too. There are some people it's dangerous to make fun of.

He pulled open a drawer and put a box of tissues on Somerton's side of the desk. Somerton gave a final, dismissive gulp and dabbed at his face with meticulous movements like a woman anxious not to disturb her make-up. It seemed a tactical moment to begin again.

'All in it. You mean?'

'Tansley-Ferrars, Haywood, that bitch; all of them. Every one a pervert.' This did seem to Bone pot calling kettle black. To everyone, however, what they did themselves was normal, a foible, while what others did was, at the very least, reprehensible.

'Tell me, Somerton, what happened; exactly.'

'What happened when?' Alarm reddened Somerton's face and he looked at the letters as he feared he must answer how they came to be written.

'When you went to Ken Cryer's, you were going to meet Alix Hamilton.'

'She said she would give me the letters if I brought the money. She was willing to sell them. She would take them to Ken's and give them to me there,' Somerton's eyes fixed still in disbelief on the file in front of Bone, 'but how is it that you have them if my wife did not give them to you?'

Bone repeated, 'They were found in Alex Hervey's flat. Alix Hamilton's flat. Why should your wife have them?'

Somerton's face convulsed. 'She wouldn't take the money. She laughed, she got into the bed, she said, "Don't you want me after all?" I said, "I want my letters," and I said this wasn't any part of the agreement between us, but I'd brought the money; she and I had a special relationship, I had needs I could never explain to my wife. Verena's delicate, she loves me. I could never hurt her, don't you see? But this was outside the relationship, bringing it here to that house. I understood she did it to give me pain, but it was . . . unsuitable. But then she said, "If you want the letters, ask your wife. I've sent them to her," and she laughed. She actually laughed. I could have killed her.'

There was a moment of surprise as it came to

him that in fact he had. The eyes changed focus; face and voice were almost apologetic.

'I saw the gun, you know, in that moment. It seemed heaven-sent.'

Bone wondered what the devil would say to that.

'It was there in the drawer just by my hand. I don't think I thought at all. It was so simple.' A fleeting satisfaction took his face, and Bone thought of the beautiful, laughing woman with perhaps a second of time to regret his joke.

There was a pause.

'I went downstairs and drank a great deal. I didn't see how I was to deal with the future, with my wife and these letters. I felt very strange. No one had heard the shot. No one knew.'

'How had she arranged the assignation?'

'She said, *Find me upstairs in ten minutes.* I had to obey her commands, of course; and of course she knew how embarrassing it would be, opening doors and being sworn at. That was her fun, and I could expect it. Still, I did find her.'

'Did you think the shot would be heard?'

'No. Until I was downstairs again I never thought of it.' Apparently Heaven, having sent the gun, might be expected to attend to such details as well. It, or the other agency, had done so. Somerton's expression, however, became disapproving once more.

'She went without me. Anne, you know. She went off without me. When I enquired I was told she had gone. Ken said that one of his thugs would drive me home, but I did not feel well; I could not

208

manage to face Verena. And it was a good move to show no reason for wishing to go. That occurred to me. No one found her, you know, for quite a long time.'

'How did "Anne" come to be at the party with you?'

'She was at the Findletters' party; I went as an aviator, with a silk scarf and my sheepskin jacket, and goggles and a helmet.'

Bone, thinking of the helmeted figures in the photographs, controlled his face and avoided Locker's significant eye. Somerton, who knew nothing of their possession of any such photographs, was not apparently conscious of the point. 'She was in armour. She may have said she was a warrior queen, or a Mistress of the Universe but we danced and talked together, and one of Ken Cryer's records was playing, so to interest her I said I was going to his party. And it did interest her. She laid her whip on my shoulder and said, "Take me there," and so I arranged to. When she called for me, however, she was in a not very distinguished black dress, of course.'

'So Miss Marsh took you home. You did not go into your house.'

'Of course not. Verena and the letters!' Once more the schoolmaster disapproved of a pupil who ought to do better. 'I got my own car and drove away.'

'Where did you drive to?'

Somerton did not appear to have heard. 'She used me as a way to see Cryer, and then deserted me. However, Miss Marsh did drive me back, after I had given an account of myself to your man here.'

Locker, stolidly philosophical at this description, accepted also that, at the time, he'd had to believe the account.

'As to where I went, I can't inform you. There was a wood. I drove into that and sat for a while. I could not see what I might do. The letters—' he stared at them and then, raising his eyes to Bone's, a tide of red seeping under his skin, said hoarsely, 'You've read them?'

Bone, his palm upward, swept it over them in a dismissive gesture. Somerton stared into the face that gave nothing away, for a full minute, breathing noticeably, the flush slowly receding.

'Yes. I suppose the police come across all sorts of such things. She told me my wife had them. She'd sent them to my wife. It was unpardonable. Every game has its rules.'

Bone thought he understood this point of view. To be humiliated in fantasy was all very well for those who wanted this kind of thing, but Somerton's wife existed in the realm of reality. That was a different world and not to be tampered with. It was quite possible that Somerton really loved his wife.

'I thought, my life is wrecked, completely over.'

Clearly Alix Hamilton's life deserved to be lost.

'After some time, I suppose, I thought of finding out what Verena . . . how she was. How – whether it had made her very ill. I feared she would have had one of her attacks and I couldn't bear the idea. She wouldn't be alone, you know.

Mrs Hasselblat is there during the day. But if Verena were ill—'

He put the mangled tissue to his mouth.

'So I thought of Jay. I didn't know about his part in this then. He was Verena's friend. He came to talk to her sometimes. She likes him! I never liked the man. Everyone is entitled to their own feelings, of course, but I am not a homosexual. I detest homosexuals. But I went there to get him to telephone her. I needed to know. But Jay was not there.' This also was an outrageous aberration on Jay's part.

'The other one, Magnus, was there. We had drinks and waited for Tansley-Ferrars. He was expected after some lecture he was giving. I talked to his wretched friend for some time, practically forgot the sort of creature he was. I don't know why I talked to him. The drink, I suppose. I hadn't eaten since breakfast.'

His general glare of injury accused the world of not looking after him in this respect.

'I talked to him about Alix. She was a friend of theirs, it turned out. I believe I had heard that. Both of them seemed to know her. I wondered how many secrets she was in the habit of confiding to her friends. It made me so angry, remembering what she had done to me—' Did he remember what he had done to her? – 'that I burst out with something, I don't know what, something about what a vicious bitch she was, not to be trusted, and I saw he was trying not to laugh. He was smirking and grimacing, and then he actually did laugh. He said Alix was so clever. Clever! And it came out why exactly she was so clever in his nasty little mind. It was the most – I was shattered. He told me she was a man. A man! He thought that funny! He thought that clever! Betrayal funny! Clever to take advantage of people's feelings when they trust you in the most profound possible way.'

Bone could not exorcise the photographs, the grovelling, grotesque figures with their helmeted heads raised blindly. Yes, you could call that trust. A fantasy could be shared with a lover, where there was trust. Where there was not, you tried a professional. Alix had posed as a lover. Then she had done two unforgivable things: punctured the fantasy by blackmail and damaged it further by turning out to be the master, not the mistress of his slave. Domination by a woman had something acceptable as a fantasy, but domination by a man – it opens a whole can of worms in male pride.

Somerton was examining his grubby cuffs with surprised distaste.

'It was a conspiracy, you know. As I told you, they were all in it. All laughing at me, because I wasn't their disgusting kind. They've nothing to laugh about. People have known how to deal with *them*!'

Bone remembered the pink triangles and the gas chambers.

'I suppose I – what is the phrase? – I saw red. Yes, I saw red.'

The drenched carpet; what remained of Magnus' face . . . Somerton seemed satisfied with his cliché.

'I really don't know what I did. I felt like

destroying the whole house, wiping it all from my mind.' He fiddled with a cuff and looked vaguely at Bone, as though he really had succeeded in erasing the uncomfortable details. Then he went on, obligingly.

'But I was still in the same position. I couldn't go home because of the letters. And I obviously couldn't get Jay to phone Verena now. You see the position I was in? When I got in my car, I drove off not knowing where to go, but I saw that disgusting creature's blood on my clothes, and I went to the sea. That must have been after some time, because it was dark. Or dusk. I have not the slightest idea where I was until then. I drove about in anguish of mind . . .'

Having once started to talk, Sutton Somerton was set to go on indefinitely. He had launched into another explanation of his dilemma when Bone broke in.

'Thank you. We understand the situation.'

There was a pause. Then Somerton said, 'I don't see how you can. I don't see how anyone can who has not been through it.'

He paused again, and leant forward peering.

'By the way, what ever happened to your head?'

CHAPTER THIRTEEN

Charlotte hurried about the flat for things she might need to pack, while Bone tried to introduce a rational note.

'Anything else you want, you can buy, chick. The Lakes are perfectly well supplied with shopping towns.'

'I know. Yes. I think I've got everything I'll want here; only do you think it'll go in that bag?'

'I don't.' Bone surveyed the garments piled on the bed. 'Better forget what you'll want and pack what you'll need.' Finally he held down the contents while she got the bag zipped shut.

'Now . . . Oh Ziggy how can I leave you?'

Ziggy, coming enquiringly in, was picked up and kissed, Charlotte's fine, mouse-blonde hair covering his struggling form.

'He'll be fine,' Bone said.

'But he'll miss me.'

'Of course he will. Cats are philosophical, though.' He took Ziggy and put him on his shoulder. 'We'll survive.'

'You'll miss me?' She was both troubled and gratified. 'But Mrs Shaw said she'd keep an eye on you.'

'Ah,' said Bone, liking this prospect. 'Will she.'

'I'll send you postcards, lots and lots. Oh, don't let me forget wellies.'

'They're downstairs by the door, ready with your boots.'

'You're terrific. You think of everything.' The door bell sounded and she went into theatrical panic, as Ziggy ran down Bone's back and leapt to the bed. 'That's them!'

The Grants were on the pavement: a cheerful, bearded man and a thin toothy woman, and Prue, who embraced Charlotte as if after weeks of absence. As Mr Grant seized upon and packed Cha's boots and wellies and bag, Bone inspected the luggage, which overflowed into the back seat. 'You've got a carful there.'

'Hardly room for Prue's earrings.' These earrings, rainbow globes on chains, looked as if she could knock herself cold by swinging her head.

Mrs Grant assured Bone she would look after Cha 'better than my own, who is tough as nails'.

'I wish we could take the cats,' Cha said. She had seen Ziggy watching up at the window.

'He'll be fine,' Prue said. 'As for ours, they *love* the cattery. Last time, Colonel Bogus didn't want to leave. When it's cold, they sleep on electric lights.' With this cryptic utterance, Prue packed herself into the car. Charlotte gave her father a convulsive hug and followed. They drove off, hands waving until out of sight.

Bone went indoors. The day was overcast, which might be the reason why the flat looked dim. It was very empty. He heard Ziggy going up to Charlotte's room, then silence. He had a slight headache, and thought of coffee and a paracetamol. He had been given the weekend off, out of turn, the Chief congratulatory although caustic about Bone's D I Y arrest of Somerton. He felt deflated.

Locker had been on Radio Kent, playing it cool. Bone, referred to by the interviewer as 'gallant', knew he would have to live that down.

He was trying to pull himself together enough to make coffee when the doorbell rang. The entry-phone said, 'Can you come with me to fetch my cat?' in a voice recognizably Grizel's. Going down-stairs, he found he was trying to finger his hair into place to hide the ugliness of his injured scalp. The dressing was off and the scar still looked, as Cha had assured him, revolting.

She stood on the step in a lavender jumpsuit. Her short, corn-coloured hair persuaded him the sun had come out. She glanced at his brow but didn't flinch.

She took his hand as they walked to the car.

Edwina laid all the military figures from the shat-tered corner cabinet in orderly fashion on a butler's tray, and carried them through to Jay in the battle room, where he was packing the soldiery in layers of felt in boxes. She had realized he would not go into the sitting-room, and had cleared it up herself.

The dog got close to his feet as she came in, and watched her.

'Thank you,' Jay said. There was no life at all in his voice or his face, which curiously was both haggard and puffy. Edwina, looking at him, thought how sad it was that, had he been deprived of a wife, he would have been supported by all the formal business of grief. As it was, losing his life's partner was a tragedy acknowledged by only a few friends; there were no crutches provided by society for a cripple of such grief.

Impulsively, she put an arm round him. He turned his head and gave her a totally automatic smile.

'You're kind. I shall get through this somehow, I know. Be better soon.' Her arm might have been hugging a stone. He turned back to his meticulous packing of the small figures. 'I can see why Magnus was fond of you.'

Finishing the layer, he covered it with felt, and then bent to pick up the dog. Edwina saw that for the moment at least he had found a better comforter. She went back to fetch the last of the soldiers.

As Grizel drove into Saxhurst, she suddenly waved and pulled up behind a car parked in High Street. The man she had waved at came over and looked dourly in at her window.

'Are you better, Dr Walsh?'

'I am going to have a printed notice hung about my neck saying "Yes, thank you".'

Bone leant across, saw the plaster on Walsh's forehead, and his bruised jaw, and said, 'Snap.'

The dark face became grimmer. Bone realized that Walsh was smiling. 'How did you catch yours?'

'Robert Bone is the policeman who was in charge of the case.'

'I fell on the suspect,' Bone said.

'How fortunate. I must have given trouble with my inadvertent theft; you could probably have done without that. I apologize. I'll undertake to be of good behaviour . . . You know, I shook that woman–man who got shot.'

'Yes. I did know;' Bone grinned, 'from the pathologist.'

'Really? Science is wonderful. Well, it's easy to say now, but I thought then that it might be a boy. The neck and throat, I think. Difficult to say where one gets an impression. Suppose it's the diagnostic eye. I saw no point in saying anything.'

'No,' said Bone. 'No point.'

Walsh nodded gravely and went off to his car.

There were times when Archangel's secretary hesitated to interrupt him even when he was doing no more than, in this case, sitting up in a hotel bed designing a necklace, but a transatlantic call from Ken Cryer merited such interruption. Archangel put down his sketchpad on the lap nearest him, which happened to be that of his minder Mary Highmountain, inserted his magic marker into the hollow of her negligée front, and took the phone. There was no sound from the cacophonous traffic of New York, fifteen floors up and with windows glazed doubly; Ken, talking from a manor in Kent across the world, sounded clearly in Archangel's ear. The couple of seconds' time lag before each answer, like an embarrassed pause, was the only sign of distance.

'*Who*? Was it any one I saw – to notice?'

A breakfast tray arrived for Archangel, and his

minder took charge of it, pouring coffee the colour of her skin into cups as white as Archangel's hair.

'Insane *sod* . . . Alex did *what*?'

He extended a hand for the coffee cup, shaking his head at cream and nodding as she indicated toast. His laugh had a slight bitterness to it.

'Not a joke he shared with me, that one, though I tell you I can think of a good few I wouldn't mind taking a whip to . . . Thanks, Ken, I'm glad to know. It helps to lay ghosts.'

But Mary Highmountain, when Archangel put down the phone and retrieved the marker from its nest of cream satin, watched his expression as he stared at the design he had drawn, and saw that the ghost of Alex Hervey was not going to be easily laid.

James Larbey, of Gryce, Fitton and Larbey, surveyed his client with a lack of enthusiasm that the client did not at all observe. The solicitor had abandoned taking notes when it became apparent that Somerton had launched on a second account of what had happened to him; this insistence on his role as a victim of circumstance had, at the first hearing of it, interested Larbey, but the second version was not going to provide anything more useful than had the first. The interview room was not warm, and Larbey moved his feet restlessly under the table, aware of tension in his cheek muscles from a desire to yawn. Sutton Somerton, with his air of outrage and the grating emphasis of his voice, was not what he would have ordered as an appetizer. The large clock on the wall behind Somerton's head had moved into a time-warp: the hands, he was sure, had not shifted for the last ten minutes.

'Why aren't you writing this down?' Somerton's forefinger stabbed at the pad in front of Larbey. 'You can't possibly remember the detail I'm giving you.' He made it sound like an act of absurd generosity.

'Very well, Mr Somerton.' Larbey picked up his biro again and wondered how it was that his client had not been a victim, rousing such a primitive desire even in his own professional breast to blot him out with anything that came to hand. All this bondage stuff – all too understandable that anyone should want to lay into Somerton, but it was difficult to associate him with S-M scenes, rather like visualizing Albert the Prince Consort as a heroin addict. Somerton had been reticent over information *there* at least, had shot his cuffs and stared as though Larbey were asking him to perform a strip tease.

'Naturally,' Somerton was saying, with unerring use of the wrong word, 'I don't expect anyone to appreciate my feelings. No one who has not been treated as I have could really enter into my situation.'

Larbey, scribbling illegibilities, wondered what Morgan Prenderghast, whom he was thinking of instructing, would make of the case, if he would find the client as boring as he did. Larbey did not know that the murderer sitting opposite had already decided his solicitor to be both inefficient and insensitive and was wondering whether to change him for another.

★　★　★

Emily Playfair ushered them in with the words, 'It's you two, how nice,' and Bone thought that to be once more one of you-two was a satisfactory thing. He was finding caution hard – keeping his hand from Grizel's shoulder when he wanted to bring her into the house. His nature and training kept him non-committal while his instinct was saying all sorts of things otherwise.

'The papers have been full of your work, Robert,' said Emily. 'Full of interest, for a change. Thank you. One gets callous about news, of course. What is interesting to me is harrowing for others, and has done your head no good at all.'

Bone put his hand over the thin scar and fading bruise. 'I'm sorry they won't let me cover it up. It's all light-and-air these days in medicine.'

'It adds to the *gallant* appearance,' Grizel remarked, idly.

'*Et tu, Brute?*'

She made an impudent face and took his hand. She said to Emily, 'Robert's coming to lunch with me—' Bone found he had, by turning his head, betrayed surprise. Emily's wicked dimples appeared – 'so we had better collect X and be away.'

'I had wanted to ask both of you to lunch myself.'

'There's nothing like being squabbled over by women,' Bone said. 'It makes me feel very gallant indeed.'

'If you're in a hurry I'll get your cat now. I've been calling him X to get him used to it, but you'll be able to name him nicely when you've observed him a while . . . I hear Mr Prestbury has cancelled visits to his house, until further notice. Trouble with the roof, they say, though he told us when we were there it had all been renewed in '87. Pity to close it in the height of the tourist season. Isn't it lucky Marian and I saw it in the spring? He's resigned from the Bench, as well. I'm an inquisitive old bag and I'd love to know what's behind that, but you're not going to tell me, are you?'

'I can't tell you anything,' said Bone.

'Grr-rr. But I was sorry about Alex Hervey.' Emily watched Grizel picking X from a consortium of kittens on the floor. 'He was an interesting writer and I much enjoyed his *Serendips*; though even the best of them weren't on a level with *A Cross on the Door*. I got that ten years ago and I've read it three times. I wish he'd written more like that. I felt he liked the people he was writing about, all the little details about their lives.'

'I'd be interested to read it,' Bone said, 'when there's time.' He remembered what Serafin had told him, of the dismissive reviews and Hervey's discouragement. Had he ever imagined his critics kneeling before him, gagged and chained?

They were leaving, with Bone carrying a small but active cat basket, and Grizel carrying *A Cross on the Door* lent to Bone, when the gate clicked and Ken Cryer ushered Jem through.

'Here are my lunch guests! I can't make these two stay, Ken; but Jem shall choose his cat, and eat ham salad and apple pie and cream.'

Bone saw Ken's response to Grizel; he saw the charm wake. She did not change. Bone thought *it will always be like that,* and would have liked to be secure enough with her not to mind when she evoked the male display.

Jem had already gone into the front room and called 'Dad! Dad!' Ken, following, paused in the doorway and said, awed, 'The Great Fur Explosion. The cats have landed.' He disappeared inside. Grizel kissed Emily and led the way down the path.

In the car, doing up her seat-belt, she leant to put a finger through the wire door of the basket on Bone's knee. 'We must do all the right things,' she said.

Before Bone could give too fervent a reply, he prudently enquired, 'Such as?'

'Oh, you know, butter on the paws. Things like that.'

As they started off, X put out a long arm through the wire mesh and gave three pats to Grizel's thigh. They drove on towards Adlingsden with Bone watching the hint of a smile in Grizel's cheek. Their silence had nothing of unease about it, and everything of promise.

THE END

A SELECTED LIST OF CRIME NOVELS
AVAILABLE FROM CORGI BOOKS

THE PRICES SHOWN BELOW WERE CORRECT AT THE TIME OF
GOING TO PRESS. HOWEVER TRANSWORLD PUBLISHERS
RESERVE THE RIGHT TO SHOW NEW RETAIL PRICES ON
COVERS WHICH MAY DIFFER FROM THOSE PREVIOUSLY
ADVERTISED IN THE TEXT OR ELSEWHERE.

*All Corgi/Bantam Books are available at your bookshop or newsagent, or can be ordered from the
following address:*

Corgi/Bantam Books,
Cash Sales Department,
P.O. Box 11, Falmouth, Cornwall TR10 9EN

Please send a cheque or postal order (no currency) and allow 60p for postage and packing for
the first book plus 25p for the second book and 15p for each additional book ordered up to a
maximum charge of £1.90 in UK.

B.F.P.O. customers please allow 60p for the first book, 25p for the second book plus 15p per
copy for the next 7 books, thereafter 9p per book.

Overseas customers, including Eire, please allow £1.25 for postage and packing for the first
book, 75p for the second book, and 28p for each subsequent title ordered.